THE WHITE WOLF TRILOGY

THE STRAY

AMANDA GEISLER

The White Wolf Trilogy book 1: The Stray

A copy of this publication can be found in the National Library of Australia.

ISBN: 978-0-6480613-8-0

Published by Ouroborus Book Services
www.ouroborusbooks.com

Visit Amanda at
www.amandageisler.com

Cover by Sabrina RG Raven: www.sabrinargraven.com
Wolf image used under license from Shutterstock.com

The Stray

Amanda Geisler

I finally did it Brodie, thanks for all your encouragement.
My only regret is that you're not here to celebrate
with me.
Rest in Peace

The wolf was never far beneath my skin, itching to be free, to run. The transformation was like a thousand needles puncturing my skin. Then the sensations became harsher, causing pain. I gave into the pain stopping myself from gasping at the feeling of fur sprouting from my skin.

Next came more pain, I winced as the first bone snapped, it was always painful. I crouched down to all fours as my back arched, my spine reshaping, fur bristled as it settled upon my skin, it was a wonder we never bled during the transformation.

Claws sprouted from the back of my fingernails, covering what was human. Then there was the uncomfortable feeling of my mouth and nose stretching. Stretching into something powerful, something dangerous. I felt my teeth sharpen, ready to rip into the flesh of some helpless deer, but that wasn't what I was shifting for. The alpha had called a meeting and I needed to know why.

The final stages of my transformation set in as my legs shortened to match the length of my arms. Both my arms and my legs thickened as powerful muscles formed beneath the skin. I could feel the gradual addition of new weight as my tail proceeded to protrude from the end of my spine.

I shook out my pure white canine fur, the glow of my golden yellow eyes reflected in the river beside me. The contacts that normally hid the tell-tale colour of my eyes had disintegrated the moment I shifted.

The wind swept through my fur as I bounded through the trees surrounding me. I drifted towards the sound of familiar footfalls as I closed in on my destination. Toby, he was kind of like my brother, my pack brother. I caught up and ran beside the sandy coloured wolf, I didn't startle him, he would have sensed me coming.

We slowed to a walk as we fought our way through thick underbrush, when we broke through the last of it, it was to find ourselves in a large, enclosed clearing. The sky was invisible above us, allowing only a small amount of light to leak through the canopy of leaves.

Several wolves sat in the clearing, all of them facing the large black wolf that sat under the small shelter that had been built a long time ago. Nobody was talking yet, the entire pack hadn't arrived, they would wait for the rest of the pack.

I knew these wolves well, they were my family ever since my parents were killed. They have taken care of me, supporting me until I was old enough to care for myself. I was an emancipated teenager now, living in my parents' old house.

Finally, the black wolf stood. This was Erik, the alpha and I despised the man, I always tried to stay as far away from him as possible but it never worked. My family were the alphas of the pack, and as one of the alpha children I might have been expected to lead; my brother was first in line, but he wasn't here.

'*Silence,*' Erik Mendez growled. There was silence; nobody disobeyed his orders, they didn't want to suffer the repercussions. '*A rogue has stumbled into our territory,*' he stated. '*This stray, has managed to get itself caught by Alec Hall.*'

'*What are we going to do with it?*' Seth asked, glancing at me briefly before looking back to his alpha. His wolf was earthen brown in colour with flecks of white.

'*For all I care Alec Hall deserves to die if he thinks he can hold a werewolf,*' Erik sneered.

My brow furrowed. '*Do you not care that we will be discovered in the process?*' I questioned.

Erik's gaze shot towards me and I felt my ears flick back under his stern gaze, my wolf telling me to submit.

'*Alec has been circling us for years, ever since he and his son came to this town.*'

'*Allowing this wolf to kill Alec is more likely to have them discover us,*' I told Erik. I knew I would get in trouble soon.

'*We risk exposure if we try to save it,*' Erik said. He seemed thoughtful though, that surprised me.

'*I can get in there,*' I announced. '*I'm close to his son, and I have Agua. Let me get this wolf out.*' Toby was staring at me as if I was crazy for making such a suggestion.

Erik continued to look thoughtful. '*If you get exposed, we won't help you,*' he told me sternly. '*Do this before the dark moon tomorrow and we will deal with the rogue afterwards.'*

I nodded. I couldn't believe that he was allowing me to do this. *'It will be done by tonight,'* I confirmed.

It was Erik's turn to nod, his was a nod of dismissal. I couldn't believe it as I quickly followed Toby out of the clearing. It was like he was a different person.

'Are you really going to do this?' Toby asked me as we ran. *'You're going to risk exposure to save a stupid rogue.'*

I shrugged. *'I'm going to try,'* I replied.

I raced past the sandy wolf rushing ahead. We branched apart as we both went to retrieve our human clothes and school bags. I wasn't expecting to run into him before reaching school, but I did. He loped up to my side as we neared the school grounds, clothes and bag in his canine mouth.

We stopped running through the trees when we heard the sounds of students on the oval beyond the forest. I dropped my bag to the ground in front of me, Toby was only a few metres away mirroring my movements.

I braced my body as I forced myself back into my human skin. Instead of snapping, my bones melted, painlessly changing back into human bones. I saw my fur sinking back beneath my lightly tanned human skin. I looked up once I was fully human, Toby was still in the throes of transforming back to human. He was newer, so it took longer for him to transform.

I pulled my clothes over my naked body. Most girls would feel awkward if they were naked in front of Toby; he wasn't exactly a nerd, but Toby had seen me shift more times than I could count even before he had shifted himself. He was the only one in the pack that I was extremely close to except for Colby.

I put a set of the usual brown contacts into my eyes, hiding the yellow while Toby dressed into human clothes and put his own set of blue contacts in making his eyes green. When he stood tall on his human legs he ran his hand through his hair, a habit of his, because he liked it messy. I however pulled a brush out of my school bag as we began walking.

There was still a fair distance to walk on human legs and, by the time we reached the fringe we were mucking around. I pushed Toby over and bounded out of the forest playfully, the grin wide on my face.

I could hear him running after me as I ran into view of students. I looked back over my shoulder; Toby was coming alright, he had determination in his eyes, but he was also grinning like an idiot.

He might have been newer, but I knew he was faster than me. It probably had something to do with his long legs. That didn't stop me from running. I had to remember to make it human speed since the humans could see us. Most of them were used to Toby and I acting like this.

I knew it when he was just about to grab me, so I side stepped as he dove past me. I laughed at him as he got quickly to his feet. I started running again, but he didn't let me get far, grabbing me unexpectedly from behind and he was not letting me go.

Toby was laughing as I tried to escape. I stomped on his foot and elbowed him in the chest behind me. He let go as I hit him.

'Ha, ha.' The sound escaped from my mouth as I

backed away.

I backed into somebody. I hadn't realised that somebody had come closer to us. I saw Toby stiffen slightly at the sight of the newcomer. All I could smell was the jealousy of the person I had walked into.

'Zac,' I announced, spinning around to face him. Zac was watching the now sheepish Toby, staring at him through stunning light brown eyes. I knew he tried not to be jealous of Toby, but I didn't think he could help it.

'What are you two doing?' Zac asked stiffly, staring Toby right in the eyes, challenging him.

'Oh, you know how it is,' Toby said with a grin. 'Mucking around with someone like Rya.'

I rolled my eyes. Toby liked riling Zac up, however, anger emanated from Zac.

'It's fine Zac,' I said, putting a hand on his arm. 'We were just having some fun.' I glanced at Toby. 'Stop being a bully.'

Toby just shrugged and walked off with a grin on his face. 'See you at lunch,' he yelled over his shoulder.

I shook my head. 'Why can't you two just get along?' I muttered more to myself then to Zac. 'It would make my life easier.'

'I just don't like him,' Zac told me, glaring after my friend. 'It's the way he looks at you.'

I laughed. Toby just had those kind of eyes. 'He's a brother to me,' I reminded Zac, not for the first time. 'You know that our parents were best friends. We were always playing together when we were little.' This was actually true, Toby had always come over to my house, he still does. 'We grew up together.'

'I know,' Zac sighed. 'It just bugs me that you're so happy around him.'

'Then you better get over it,' I told him. 'Because Toby isn't going anywhere, anytime soon.' Zac was still watching Toby, who had just reached the school buildings. I sighed. 'I'm going to class.'

***

My teacher arrived just as I sat down in my seat. He was whistling, surprising me and the rest of the class. Mr Hammond was usually such a sour person.

'I know that you're all interested in the werewolf claims that were on the news today,' he announced. 'So, we're going to spend a few days studying the werewolf myths and legends. There are many different werewolf mythologies, so I would like you to choose one and write a paper about it, to be finished by Wednesday next week.'

There was a collective sigh throughout the room. I had sighed too, but for a different reason. A dark moon was coming before the due date and that meant one less night to work on the paper.

'But how do we know which one is correct?' a student from the back of the classroom asked.

Mr Hammond looked at the student. 'We can't know for sure until the lead researcher is able to communicate with the werewolf they have in custody. Then, early next week, Alec Hall has allowed me to organise a little excursion to his laboratory. He should be able to tell us about all the different mythologies.' Mr Hammond paused. 'After he manages to talk to the werewolf of course.' I sensed Hammond glance at me.

I hid my horror. Not only had they almost discovered us, they also intended to find out our secrets. It was a good thing that I would be getting the wolf out of there, I just didn't know how yet.

We were allowed to spend the rest of the lesson researching our papers on the internet with the laptops we used for class. I already knew that I was going to base my paper on the mythology that was real.

Werewolves were descended from the Greek King Lycaon and his children. They angered the God Zeus by serving him the flesh of Nyctimus, Lycaon's youngest son. I of course had to limit the details I added to the ones discussed in the human version of our histories. I would have to leave out our connection to witches and the fact that Lycaon also had a daughter included in the curse.

The bell rang and we began to pack up our things for our ten-minute break before our next class. Normally, it was just enough time to swap books over at the lockers and have a bite to eat, but luckily, today I had a free period and an entire hour to myself.

I almost ran to my locker to grab a bit of food, I kept my history books and my laptop. Zac had the period off as well and most of the time we would sit out on the field to study. However, Zac liked to get distracted and unknowingly test my self-control.

I walked through the hallways that were busy with students making their way to their next class and left the building just as the next bell rang, walking to the tree Zac and I sat under during our free periods together. It was a place we could just enjoy each other's company, sometimes studying, and other times doing a lot more than that. When I was with him sometimes it felt like I was melting. I always had to stop him, because I was scared I might transform. I didn't know if I would be able to stop myself. I knew when I was angry I still sometimes had trouble stopping myself from shifting.

I had just settled when Zac arrived, his laptop resting open on his forearm, it had probably just been used in his last class. He sat down close to me, his hip resting against mine. For a quick moment, it was all I thought about.

'When do you have history?' I asked him. I couldn't remember if he had it today; stupid two-week timetables.

'Not till after lunch,' he replied. He was more comfortable without Toby around. His voice was softer and he was more relaxed when it was just us.

'We're studying werewolf mythologies,' I told him. 'He wants us to choose the one we think is the real one and write a paper on it.'

He sighed. 'When is it due?'

'Wednesday. You could come over to mine and we can work on it together?' I suggested.

'Sure. I'll check with my dad for some of his information on werewolf history.' He was silent for a moment. 'Enough about school work,' he said, pushing his laptop off his knees.

He pulled me closer and put his arms around me. He kissed me deeply, his lips parting mine. When we finally broke apart we were gasping for breath. His lips travelled from my mouth down to my neck, my skin tingled in response.

I gasped again at the tingling feeling they gave me. I put my hand around his neck and pulled his lips back to mine. He made a joke of resisting, but it was feeble and soon our lips connected once again. Our school work was forgotten and my self-control was dwindling. Soon, I would have to pull away again. Zac lowered me down on to my back, his lips still pressed against mine.

I knew that it was going too far, but I couldn't bring myself to break away. Even when his mouth wasn't on mine, it was somewhere pressed against my skin and all I could do was respond. He ran his hand down my side, his hands sliding higher. I lost all control. My hands began to burn with the first signs of transformation. One hand dug into the ground beside me.

Someone shoved Zac off of me, angering him until he saw it was his best friend, Dylan Andrews. He was always interrupting the moments I had with Zac. This time, however, I was grateful. Zac leaped to his feet to mock fight Dylan while I got myself back under control. I sat up and looked clenching my hands closed, hiding the claws that had appeared. I took a deep breath and they disappeared. Boys, I thought, looking up at them. I shook my head.

'Righto boys,' I said to them in the fake motherly voice I used every time this happened. 'Do I need to break up this fight, or will you save me the hassle?'

As always, they stopped mid wrestle, looked at me, then sat up and pulled the usual innocent look. I had to stop myself from laughing. They looked like pups when they got caught doing something naughty. The laughter erupted in the end, bubbling over so that in the end the boys joined me.

'So anyway,' Dylan said. 'What are you doing?' He glanced at our discarded laptops and books and grinned.

'We were supposed to be studying,' I said in an accusing tone. 'But somebody got us a little bit distracted.'

Dylan laughed. 'Yep, that's our Zac.' He dodged Zac when he tried to push Dylan over again. 'Anyway, you're lucky I butted in. You guys were getting a bit carried away. I recommend finding a room.'

We spent the rest of the free period talking about the paper that Mr Hammond had assigned us. Dylan thought he might write about the French history of werewolves while Zac decided to wait to see what his dad said. Soon the bell rang and students started piling out of the buildings.

I grabbed my stuff and stood to leave. 'I'm gonna go hang out with Agua,' I told the boys.

Zac moved toward me for a quick kiss. 'See you this arvo.' I nodded briefly in response.

As I walked towards the cafeteria I heard Dylan speak. 'Dude, you're so whipped.' I heard the responding thud as Zac tackled him. I walked faster shaking my head at the immaturity going on behind me.

The cafeteria wasn't far from where I had been sitting with Zac. It was just a couple of hundred metres away, not that you could miss such a large building, especially when there were hordes of students heading towards it.

Inside the cafeteria there were students lining up, waiting for their chance to get food. This was around the edge of the room. There were fridges and hotboxes filled with food and drinks just waiting to be consumed by the masses that lined up during lunch.

The rest of the building was filled with thirty or so tables of differing sizes, allowing groups to choose tables depending upon the amount of people that would be sitting there. Even in a town as small as this there were lines drawn between the students. There were about five hundred students all together, they were divided up into sporty kids, like Zac and Dylan. Then there were the popular kids that thought they ruled the school, the computer geeks, the nerds and the outsiders. We also had a group of dance and drama geeks.

Then of course there were us supernatural kids.

The young werewolves in the pack stuck together, making sure everybody was okay, and this is where I found Agua and Toby, chatting comfortably with Mira, Max, Liam and Brian. The rest of the school labelled us as the rich kids. They knew that we were the old families in town and that all of us had grown up fairly close.

I placed my tray on the table next to Agua's and climbed onto the bench. *'I heard you have a mission,'* Agua said silently, she could communicate with us mentally, since she was supernatural too. This was how we usually discussed our secret lives at school.

I nodded, knowing that the other wolves at the table were listening. *'You and I need to get that wolf out tonight,'* I told her. I shovelled the spaghetti into my mouth. One benefit of mind speaking was that we could talk while we ate.

'Do you know how yet?' she asked me.

'I have an idea.' I explained the idea I had come up with while I was outside with Dylan and Zac.

'What do you want us to do?' Mira asked me.

I looked up at her. *'Nothing,'* I replied. *'You would just get in the way. Just me and Agua,'* I explained.

'I'm coming,' Toby stated. *'I'm not letting you go near that scientist without back up.'*

I shook my head, slightly so the humans didn't notice. *'Zac doesn't like you. He likes Agua. You can meet us in the forest,'* I compromised.

'Us too,' Mira announced.

I shook my head. *'No,'* I said firmly. *'You haven't turned yet. You would just get in the way.'*

They pouted. I gave them a stern look, and after a

few moments they looked down at the table in front of them, submissive. I might not be alpha of the pack but I was still higher than them.

I was slightly startled when Zac sat down on my other side. He never really sat with us, he had his soccer team to sit with. But then I saw that Zac was watching Toby. I sighed. *Seriously?* 'What's up?' I asked him casually, ignoring the fact that everybody at the table had gone tense. None of them liked Zac very much. However I could sense amusement emanating from Toby. This was going to be fun.

'Mum and Dad are going away for the weekend,' Toby announced, looking at me. 'They were wondering if I could stay at your place tomorrow night.' He glanced at Zac, while Toby's face was serious, amusement rolled off him in waves, but he hid this fact from Zac.

I glared at him slightly. 'That's fine,' I told him lightly. His parents were werewolves of course, but sometimes they wanted to have the dark moon night to themselves, or more importantly Toby didn't want to spend it with his parents. Zac however didn't seem okay with it. He was glaring at Toby, but I was glad that he chose not to comment.

I glanced at Zac. 'So, when are you going to talk to your dad?' I asked him.

'I'm supposed to help him out this afternoon,' Zac replied, almost uneasily.

'Can we come?' I asked.

Agua spoke up. 'Yeah,' she said. 'It would be great to hear what your dad says.'

'Just you two,' Zac said. We nodded. 'That's fine

then.' He got up and walked away.

I smacked Toby lightly on the shoulder. He ducked, a grin on his face. 'Why did you do that?' I asked, glaring slightly.

He shrugged, still grinning. 'It was worth it. That guy is such an idiot.'

I ignored his comment. 'It gives us an in with Alec and right now we need that.'

'What happens if this plan of yours doesn't work?' Toby asked, suddenly serious. 'Then you and Agua get locked up and there won't be anything we can do about it.'

'We'll be fine,' Agua told him. 'It's an easy plan, not anything that I haven't done before.'

Toby raised his eyebrows at her. 'You've broken into a government facility before?' he asked sceptically.

'No,' Agua replied. 'I was talking about everything else.'

'I still don't like this plan,' Toby said. 'You heard what Erik said, they won't be able to protect you if you get caught.'

'We need to protect our secret,' I told him firmly. 'I know that it's risky but we need to do this tonight.' Toby stood up to leave. 'Just meet us in the forest with a med kit,' I told him. 'We might need it.'

'Fine,' he said, the bell ringing just as he disappeared. I sighed and got to my feet with every other student in the room.

***

We met up with Zac at my locker after classes finished

and quickly made our way out of the school. I had my school bag with me but it was pretty much empty except for a few sets of clothes, a pen and a notebook. I never went anywhere without a spare set of clothes, but it wasn't me that would be needing them today.

It took almost an hour to get to the lab. It was past the outskirts of town, away from people that experiments may disturb, since they didn't just study werewolves. Apparently there were other things here too, but Zac couldn't tell me what they were.

The lab towered over us. It looked kind of like a university except a little bit smaller. There were metal fences around the edge and a guard at the open gate. They waved us through; they knew Zac.

Zac knew the way to his dad's part of the place so he easily led us through the corridors. I did my best to remember the way out, for the mission and for the sake of keeping my wolf under control, I always had to know the escape route.

Finally we came to the last door. Zac put in the code 2, 9, 4, and 8. The door opened allowing us access. Zac's father, Alec Hall, was the only one inside. He looked like an older version of Zac except his skin was paler, probably because he was always here and didn't seem to be as muscular. He was brainy while Zac was sporty.

My eyes fell onto the cage in the corner of the room. A small wolf was resting inside, a grey wolf, its right hind leg was slick with blood, I could smell the infection starting in the wound. It was a wonder that it was still in wolf form, the bullet must be lodged inside the leg, otherwise it would have healed by now.

I cautiously reached my mind over to the wolf and forced my way into its thoughts. 'I'm here to help you,' I told the wolf. The wolf's eyes snapped open and it turned to face me. I saw it take a deep breath. 'I'm like you,' I said, trying to reassure it. Understanding came across the link. I placed my bag next to the door. *Wait till the coast is clear then make a run for it, there are clothes for you in my bag.'*

'So, what have you found out about it?' I asked Alec, the question had burst from my mouth.

'Nothing,' Alec responded. 'It still hasn't turned back into human form. All we know is that it's female.'

'Then how do you know it's a werewolf?'

'We ran a DNA test,' he replied. 'It came back with equal amounts of human and wolf DNA.'

'We have to write a paper about what we believe to be the history of werewolves,' Zac explained to his father. 'We wanted to know what you think before we start.'

I put on a big smile. 'Maybe a little tour first?' I suggested. I glanced at Agua. She was nodding eagerly. That was her signal. I saw her hand move only the slightest amount, it could have just been a muscle twitch. Out of the corner of my eye I saw the cage silently unlock itself.

'Sure thing,' Alec said. 'We can talk about it on the way.' I stooped down to pick up the bag. 'Just leave your stuff here,' Alec told me, that's what I had been hoping he would say. 'Most of the time nobody comes in here except for me.' So far so good.

I followed them out the door, giving the wolf the

slightest of nods. *'Meet you in the forest,'* I told her. *'I will find you.'* Acknowledgement came across the link.

Alec took us around his area of the facility. He showed us the data they had received on the werewolf DNA, along with a cure that they were trying to develop. It made me even happier that the wolf would soon be safe.

Finally we came to a room, it looked like a printer had exploded. The walls were covered in printed out pages, photographs and newspaper clippings. 'This is the stuff you will need for your paper,' Alec announced. 'We have been researching all the known mythologies and legends regarding werewolves. Unfortunately the web is flooded with unreliable information, so it has been quite the task trying to find the more reliable sources,' Alec explained.

'What are the most likely?' Agua asked. She looked genuinely curious; she was such a good liar. Or she was just curious to know if they were on track.

'We have narrowed it down to three possibilities.' Alec tells her. 'Greek, French or Native American,' he clarified. 'We hope that the werewolf can shed some light on it when she shifts back.'

Just three huh. And one of them was the correct mythology, or at least as close as the humans have ever gotten. 'Why do you think these ones could be true?' I asked.

'They discuss the beginning of the werewolf race,' Alec said. 'A lot of the mythologies we came across merely jumped straight into giving us a rundown about what they believe werewolves are. These ones were able to give reasons for the beginning of werewolves as well as giving historical insight to the species.'

'So personally,' I began, 'how do you feel about werewolves?'

'Until now I felt like I was always chasing my tail in my research,' he stated. *Did he mean to use that metaphor?* 'I finally found something to work with, proof of the existence of werewolves in our world,' he continued. 'Are they a threat? Maybe,' he considered. 'But maybe werewolves stayed secret this long because they are hiding within society. Assimilating, if you want to call it that.'

I had to admit it was a well thought out answer. 'If they were a threat wouldn't they have been found out already?' I suggested. 'I mean. I know it's a beast, but wouldn't there be some human in there too.' Had to keep up the ruse. I hated calling myself a beast, that wasn't what we were; wasn't what we did.

'That's why I must continue my studies,' Alec agreed. 'I'm sorry I couldn't be more help for your paper.'

'That's fine,' Agua and I said together.

'You gave us stuff to think about,' Agua finished.

We started heading back to the original lab where I hoped there was no longer a wolf in the cage. Sure enough, the cage was wide open when we entered, my bag had moved but only slightly, but nobody seemed to notice that.

Alec swore and hit a blue button on the wall. Sirens started to go off everywhere and I clapped my hands to my ears. It was so loud, and the supernatural hearing didn't help. 'Let's get out of here,' I shouted to Agua over the noise, she nodded.

I told Zac that we were going to head home. He nodded but I'm not entirely sure that he heard me. I grabbed my bag and left the lab with Agua a step behind me. I used my sense of smell to follow the wolf's scent. I was glad to see it was heading for the exit.

We followed it all the way to the front gate, the scent headed into the forest. She had escaped. The guard watched us as we left. We made a show of walking down the path until we were out of sight, then we ducked into the trees after checking to make sure that nobody was watching us.

When we found the wolf, it was to find it facing off with Toby. The wolf was growling. It looked like Toby was trying to talk to it, the medical kit sat on the ground. I rushed between them as the wolf stepped towards him. 'It's okay,' I told the wolf. 'He's a friend.'

Recognition flicked across the wolf's face and she relaxed. Slowly I moved closer, Toby following close behind me. I inspected her wounded leg. 'The bullet's still lodged in your leg.' I told the wolf. 'That's why you're not healing.' I stared into the wolf's eyes. 'I need you to shift back. It will be easier to fix.' The wolf looked cautiously around at the three people surrounding her. 'It alright. You're safe.' I looked up at Toby. 'Alec has DNA evidence,' I told him.

Toby nodded in understanding. 'I will get onto it when I get to a computer.' Toby's family were the computer wizards of the pack. They'd learnt how to hack into all sorts of things so we could destroy any evidence of our existence.

'I'm going to get this bullet out.' Toby handed me the

medical kit. The wolf had listened to our conversation. 'It's okay,' I told her again. 'You can trust us.'

The wolf didn't respond. She collapsed, turning back into human form a few seconds later. I swore, throwing open the kit and pulling out the things I needed. 'Agua, keep her alive.'

Agua crouched down and put a glowing hand on the raven-haired girl on the ground in front of us. 'She's okay,' Agua told me. 'I think the exhaustion took over.'

I didn't have a chance to sigh with relief, I was too busy pulling the bullet out of her leg with tweezers. It was a large bullet for such a small leg, probably a rifle. The needle and thread was next, a few quick, neat stitches later and the wound was closed up, it would heal now.

Something snapped, my head turned in the direction of the lab. The humans were tracking her. 'We have to go,' I told the others. 'Now.' I picked the girl up in my arms and Agua grabbed the medical kit. 'Let's go,' I said. 'They're coming.'

Toby may have been faster than me, but my hearing was definitely better than his. They weren't too far away. We bolted, I couldn't run at full speed with the extra weight and Agua couldn't run as fast as us. The humans were closing in.

I stopped in front of a tree. 'Go,' I told Toby. 'I'll hand her up.'

Toby was quick to leap into the tree. I passed the small girl up to Toby. I jumped up and climbed to a branch higher than him and he passed the girl to me. We continued in this fashion until we reached the top, Agua was climbing up behind us, she had hidden the medical kit in the bushes below us. By the time the humans came into view we were safely hidden at the top amongst the leaves.

I had the still unconscious girl back in my arms. I peered through the branches down to the ground below. The guards had dogs with them that were sniffing the trail. The humans were looking around, probably expecting to find us. I sighed, Zac was with them.

The girl gasped loudly as she lurched awake. I gripped her tighter and clamped my hand over her mouth. I stopped myself from gasping in pain as her fangs clamped onto my hand. *'Stop!'* I yelled silently.

I continued to hold my hand in front of her mouth and she continued to bite, blood seeping out around her teeth. I glanced down at the ground, the dogs were staring up at us. I closed my eyes banging the back of my head against the tree behind me.

I looked over at Toby. *'I'm going to lead them away,'* I told him, allowing Agua and the girl to hear me as well.

'No,' he stated. *'It's too dangerous.'*

'They're going to find us.' I looked at the girl. *'Can you keep quiet?'* She nodded in response. I removed my hand from her mouth. I glanced at Agua. *'Disguise me.'*

Agua didn't answer, instead she placed her hand on my head. I felt my body go stiff as the magic coursed through me. I braced myself, eyes closed. I could only just hear the humans talking about us being in the tree.

Then the magic was gone. I opened my eyes, I was smaller, not much smaller, but I was smaller. I could see black hair sitting on my shoulders where blonde hair had been only moments before, and my skin was lighter, almost pale.

I looked down at the ground again, letting the girl go. They had a rifle, a bloody rifle. I took a deep breath. *'Take her to my house,'* I told them. *'I'll meet you there.'*

I didn't give Toby a chance to protest. I jumped down out of the tree, landing a few metres away from the humans and their dogs. The humans were startled, staring briefly at me, then the tree I had come out of. I bolted.

I heard the gunshot not long after I ran. I rolled, out of habit. I heard the bullet sail past me as I came back to my feet, and took off. I heard the running feet behind me. I ran as fast as I could in this human form, it wasn't super-fast but it was still faster than a human.

Then I heard the dogs. I tried to run faster, but they were faster than my two-legged form. I turned on them, stopping suddenly, and I growled at them, a ferocious growl. The dogs' tails drooped, falling between their legs as they ran back in the direction they had come. The humans came back into sight as their dogs ran past them. I turned and continued to run.

I couldn't lose them. It didn't matter how fast I ran they were never too far behind me, how the hell could these people track me so easily. It wasn't night time yet and none of the trees had enough leaves to hide me. I wish they would just give up.

I ran until darkness fell, only then was I able to hide

up in the trees. As the sun disappeared beyond the horizon I climbed the nearest tree, taking myself up to the top. Then, very quietly, I started making my way back to fringe of the forest, leaping silently from tree to tree.

The humans were walking underneath me as I leapt to another tree, grabbing the trunk with my claws before landing softly on another branch. I stayed silent as they continued to follow my old tracks, when they disappeared, I jumped back down to the ground.

I landed in a crouch, looking in the direction that the humans went. I stood up, turning. 'Zac.'

I froze. He was staring at me, squinting like he was trying to work out who I was. 'Do I know you?' he asked. Of course that was when the spell chose to wear off. I sighed as the magic made my skin tingle and my disguise started to disappear.

I turned away, it was dark enough that he couldn't see my face. I wasn't expecting to the wolf to fly past me and attack. 'Erik,' I shouted, running back after the wolf. 'Leave him alone.' Erik had pinned a terrified looking Zac on the ground.

'He knows who you are,' the wolf said into my head.

'Let him go.'

'I'm protecting you.'

'You're not protecting me by killing people!' I growled. 'If we want to stay secret then you have to stop killing humans. It's what brought them all here in the first place.'

The wolf turned on me. I saw Zac's relief that the wolf was no longer on him, he hadn't seen me yet. *'Why should I listen to you?'* he asked. *'I'm the alpha of this pack.'*

'Not for much longer.' I knew this would get me in trouble.

The wolf dove for me and Zac scurried away as I retaliated. I could see the confusion in his eyes as he finally saw my face in the darkness. He hadn't seen me transform. Erik hadn't expected me to fight back. I pinned him.

'Let me deal with this,' I stated.

His jaw closed around the flesh of my arm. I almost cried out in pain as his fangs closed on bone. A moment later he was leaning over me, my blood dripping from his mouth. *'I should kill you right now.'*

'Then do it,' I told him. 'I won't have to see you destroy everything we stand for.'

I took one last chance. I pulled myself out from under Erik as quickly as I could, wincing as my transformation stretched my wound. Despite my injured arm I got my clothes off before they could rip. I would need something to get back into.

I was surprised he waited for me to transform. Maybe he knew that I couldn't win, just like I knew. I was already hurt. The wolf almost seemed to smirk at me. I went for the attack barrelling into the black wolf. It wasn't my intention to win, it was my intention to stop him from killing Zac.

He rolled with me when he was knocked off his feet. I closed my fangs around anything I could sink them into. I could taste his blood in my mouth. He ended up standing over me, stronger and for the moment, more dominant.

His paw was on my canine chest, claws stretching, digging into my skin. He closed his jaw around what would be my bicep a second later and tore away the flesh before I could pull away. *'Consider yourself warned,'* Erik growled. *'Now deal with this human before you get us all killed.'*

I didn't move until he was gone. Even then I only partially relaxed in response to his absence. I forced myself to take human form. Blood coated my right arm, it was practically shredded. I was glad my other arm was fine. It meant that I could push myself up without screaming in pain.

It wasn't until I was fully clothed again that I turned around to face Zac. He hadn't moved. I wasn't sure if he was afraid, in shock or what but he was starting directly at me as if I was an alien. Or a werewolf I supposed.

'Zac?' I could hear the uncertainty in my own voice.

He flinched at the sound of his name. 'Who are you?'

I sat down beside him, keeping a distance between us. 'I'm the same person you've been dating for the last year.'

'You seem to have left a few parts out.'

'Not something that I can change,' I responded, trying not to let the emotions I smelled get to me. 'I wouldn't want to anyway.'

My wounds were starting to itch as they started healing. 'You like not belonging to yourself.'

'Whoa,' I exclaimed. 'Whatever you think you know about werewolves is probably wrong. Most of us, are perfectly in control of our wolf side.'

'What about that black one?' Zac looked in the direction Erik had gone. 'He seemed a lot like I'd expect.'

'He's one of the exceptions,' I told him. 'There aren't very many like him.'

'How many of you are there?' he asked.

'In town, or in the country?' I responded. The wounds on my arm finished sealing shut, my skin settling back to normal. 'Thank god. I hate healing.' I used the shirt to wipe the blood off my arm.

'You healed already?' he asked, staring at my arm with a small amount of amazement.

'Compared to the injuries I've had that was nothing. He only left me mobile because he didn't want to have to deal with you.'

'Are you going to kill me?' he asked.

'Never,' I told him flatly. I could see the question in his eyes. 'Honestly I have no idea what to do with you. Under pack law, if you are a threat to us, we are justified to kill you and not be killed for taking a human life.'

'What does that mean?' he questioned.

'It means that if you intend to tell people about me then don't because Erik will kill you,' I told him. 'He might be psychotic but he is trying to protect us.'

'You're not what I thought,' Zac said. 'You were supposed to be normal.'

I looked at him. 'I am normal,' I scolded. 'I'm just not human.' I got to my feet. 'Come on.'

'Where are you taking me?' he asked, I heard the instant fear in his voice.

'Do you want to get out this forest?' I stated flatly. He didn't move. 'I'm not going to hurt you. We're going back to my house so I can check in. Otherwise they're going to track me down and now it's dark it will be easier to slip past your father's people.' I started walking and I could hear him rush to catch up.

'You're scared of my father?'

'I'm afraid of being put in a cage,' I retorted. 'But your father is no friend of mine.'

'Is that why you came with me today?' he asked, trying to keep up with my pace. 'To save your friend.'

'She's not my friend,' I told him. 'Right now, she's a stranger that's entered pack territory. I just had to get her out before she killed someone.'

'Do you know where you're going?' Zac asked suddenly.

'I grew up in this forest,' I told him. 'If I didn't know where I was something would be wrong with me.' I noticed he changed the subject every time the word killing came up.

'So, you've been like this a long time?'

'I was born this way,' I answered. 'I wasn't bitten and turned into a werewolf.'

'So you're scared of my father because he might lock you in a cage?'

'You'd think somebody who was terrified would stay quiet,' I stated just loud enough for him to hear. He didn't respond so I answered him. 'I'm not afraid of the cage.'

'Then what?'

'I'm afraid of what will happen after that,' I admitted. 'My blood is older than most, which makes me more dangerous if I can't keep myself under control.'

'How old are you?' he asked. 'Are you even a teenager?'

God, he asked a lot of questions. 'No, I'm not a teenager,' I answered. 'Technically I'm younger. My blood is older because of my family and us being the oldest bloodline of werewolves.'

'So...'

'My family were the first to become werewolves.' He opened his mouth. 'Enough questions,' I said before he could speak. 'I have to deal with this before they go crazy.'

'With what?' I shushed him, as we left the forest. The street was dark except for a single light post. I avoided the light so nobody would notice the blood on my shirt if they looked out the window. I opened the unlocked door.

Arms wrapped around me a moment later. 'I was about to come looking for you,' Toby stated. 'Are you okay?' He hadn't noticed Zac yet.

'I'm fine,' I answered. 'It took me a while to lose them, then I had a run in with Erik.'

'What, why?' He was shocked. 'The mission was a success.'

'I ran into another problem.' I looked over my shoulder at Zac. 'I didn't exactly get caught but...'

Toby followed my gaze. 'He knows?' Toby asked.

'Unfortunately,' I responded.

'How'd he take it?' Toby asked.

I shrugged. 'Not sure yet,' I answered. 'Too early to tell. He's just terrified we're going to kill him.'

'We could do that?' Toby said, looking over my shoulder with a serious expression on his face.

Toby smirked when we heard Zac's heart beat a little faster. 'No one's killing him.'

'I guess you're a werewolf too?' Zac asked.

'Believe what you want. I could be anything.'

'You're not helping,' I told him. I looked at Zac. 'Get inside.' He didn't move. 'Nobody's going to hurt you.'

He hesitated a moment longer before allowing me to close the door behind him. Something crashed in the lounge. 'You guys might want to get in here,' I heard Agua call.

We practically flew around the section wall that blocked us from the lounge. The girl was in wolf form again, her grey tail bushy and erect. She was ready to defend herself if she had to. She growled when she saw us.

'Stop it,' I told her. 'Do you want somebody to hear you?'

The response I got was another growl, it was lower in volume though. I stood up as tall as possible. Then I glared down into her eyes. I was more dominant here, especially with her. 'How many times do I have to tell you?' I asked, a growl in my voice. 'I'm trying to help you. Now stand down.'

Toby ducked his head, he was submissive to me as well. He listened. I walked towards the grey wolf. Her legs buckled beneath her, her wolf forcing her into submission. 'Human form, now,' I told the cowering wolf.

The wolf looked up at me, but not in my eyes, and whined. I crouched down beside her. 'Now!' I growled. 'It's a hell of a lot easier to talk if we're both human.'

Her body was quivering, her wolf forcing her to obey. She scurried backwards when she was human again, putting as much distance between us as she could. 'What did you do to me?'

'In this territory, everyone listens to me,' I told her. 'I'm stronger, I'm older and in this town, I'm definitely more dominant then you.'

'I've never been able to pull it back, I've always had to sleep it off.'

'What's your name?'

'Maya.' She answered.

'How long has it been since you turned?' I asked her.

'A month.'

'Were you bitten?' I demanded. She was looking at the ground in front of me.

'What?'

'Were you bitten?' I repeated. 'Did you get bitten by a wolf?'

'No,' she said. 'I don't know how it happened.'

I glanced at Toby, he looked away from me quickly. 'She could have been lost in the system,' he suggested, he didn't meet my eyes.

I looked back at the girl. She looked maybe fourteen. Slightly earlier than normal. 'Where are your parents?'

'Dead.' She stated.

'You killed them.'

'I… I don't know,' she whimpered. 'I can't remember.'

I looked at Agua. She nodded once and moved forward. The girl shrank under her gaze. 'My friend is going to access your memories. Can she do that?'

'Why?' the girl stammered.

'We need to know if you've tasted human blood. It will… alter the learning process.'

'Rya, she needs to be willing for me to do this.'

'I don't think we're going to get that right now,' I informed her. I looked at the girl. 'Do you know what tomorrow is?'

'No,' her voice quivered. 'I don't know anything. Just that I keep turning into a wolf.'

'Because you haven't been taught how to control it,' I told her. 'Don't worry, I was just like you. I was probably worse.'

'How long have you been a freak?'

'You're not a freak,' I told her. 'You were born this way, if you weren't bitten. You've reached maturity and your wolf has awakened.'

'How long?' she asked again.

'Six years,' I answered.

'What about him?' she was looking at Toby.

'Just a few months,' I confirmed. 'He's still learning, but unlike you he's been prepared for it.'

'The council won't do anything to her,' Agua said. 'Even if she has taken a life.'

'I know,' I answered. 'I can't teach her unless Erik allows her to stay.'

'Who's Erik?' she asked.

'The alpha,' I told her. 'He's the only werewolf that won't listen to me.'

'He's the one that hurt you?' she asked.

I nodded. 'Tomorrow is a dark moon,' I told her. 'The first time you transformed was a dark moon. It's the only night that it's impossible to control the shift. We also don't remember what happens, while we don't have control.'

'What do I do?' she seemed to breath more rapidly.

'We lock you away.'

'So I'm going into another cage.'

'You don't have a choice,' I told her firmly. 'At least you'll be let out of this one once you wake up. If it makes you feel better the two of us will be locked up too.'

'I don't want to go through that again,' she said. 'I don't want to transform.'

'You don't have a choice,' I said again. I tried a reassuring tone. 'It won't be as hard this time.'

'It helps if you don't fight it,' Toby added. 'It's the only time you should let it take over.'

'Toby,' I said. 'That's something to talk about tomorrow when we have an hour before moonrise.'

'Who are you people?' the girl asked.

'The ones that saved you,' I told her. 'I have a spare room that you're welcome to stay in, until we get you settled with a pack family.'

'And if I don't want your help.'

'Then you won't learn how to control your abilities and you are more than likely going to be killed tomorrow night because you won't have a place to contain yourself.'

'I think I'll stay,' she said quickly.

I heard the front door close. 'Hall?' Toby said flatly. 'He's gone.'

'Let him go,' I stated. 'We can't keep him forever, if he's going to tell, he's going to tell.'

'I hope you know what you're doing,' Agua stated.

So do I. 'I don't know. I wouldn't mind not having to hide.' I gave my two serious friends a joking smile. 'Let's just go to sleep,' I said after a moment's silence. 'We'll deal with him tomorrow.'

ZAC HALL

I expected them to come after me. I expected her to come after me. I practically ran home, it wasn't that far from her house. What was I going to do? I'd been lied to and a part of me understood why. That was the worst part. I understood why she'd lied to me.

I closed the door behind me once I finally managed to get it open. I leaned against it, breathing shakily. What were they going to do with me? I wasn't supposed to find out about them. That much was clear.

I was glad my father was still out looking for the werewolf. God, she's a thief too. What else had she done to protect her secret? How was I supposed to trust her? She was a freaking werewolf. I pulled myself away from the door and went into my room, locking my bedroom door.

I couldn't sit still. My thoughts were racing through everything that had happened tonight. How had they saved that wolf? They weren't even in the room when it escaped and the camera footage, that must have been them too.

Toby was a werewolf too. How many of them were

there? Was Agua a werewolf or was she something else? Something else, I guessed, remembering about her accessing that girl's memories. That werewolf's memories.

She said that she had been just like the wolf, or worse. What did she mean? Unable to control the shift, or tasted human blood. Maybe both. She apparently had good control over it now though. And the way the kid had reacted when she walked over to her. The way she cowered under her stare. The way Toby had reacted to it to. She was stronger then him. Every werewolf listened to her, except one.

I should tell somebody, I should tell my father. What would he do to her? He would lock her in a cage, that much was obvious. What would happen after that? He would try to cure her. He would take away that side of her, she would be human again.

I heard the front door open and close. For a moment I thought it would be one of them, then there was a knock on my door. I made myself seem calm. 'Did you find your wolf?' I asked, opening the door.

'No,' my father responded. 'Somebody helped it. We found evidence of first aid. They took the bullet out of its leg. It could be human and a hundred miles away by now.'

Or a few hundred meters. 'That's too bad.' I wanted to tell him, I wanted him to cure her, he could make her human. But for some reason I couldn't get the words out.

'Are you alright?' He seemed to notice my desire.

'Yeah,' I said. 'Just tired.' Not the words I was meant to say.

'Get some sleep,' he said. 'You have a big game on Saturday night.' Game? Right, soccer. I closed the door after my father had walked away, I laid down on my bed. Sleep. How the hell was I going to sleep?

RYA GARCIA

I probably shouldn't have done it the way I did. I didn't want to terrify him any more then he already was. 'Did you tell him?' I asked, cornering Zac at his locker after school. He had been avoiding me all day.

'What are you talking about?' Zac asked.

I grabbed his wrist. He flinched but I didn't let go. I pulled him to the closest empty classroom and closed the door. 'Did you tell your father what I am?' I almost growled.

'What happens if I say yes?' he said.

'Then I have to leave,' I told him flatly. 'It wouldn't be safe for me anymore.'

'I didn't tell him,' he told me. 'But I should, if he could make you human again.'

'I've never been human.' He flinched at the anger in my voice. 'And I don't want to be human.' I walked towards the door. If I hadn't been so angry, I would have let him, but I grabbed his wrist before he could touch me. I spun him around and pinned him against the wall. 'I'm going to leave now, and I will talk to you about this when I'm not so dangerous to be around. Until then, tell no one.'

I let him go and walked out of the room. I had to ignore the stares I was getting as I left the school hallway. Zac and I had never had a fight since we started dating. I took a deep breath, I just had to make it to the forest, then I could run.

ZAC HALL

Despite what she said I followed her, ignoring my classmates' glances. I stopped at the main door. I could see her across the oval, heading towards the trees. She hit the tree line I wasn't so far away that I didn't see her skin ripple. She was a wolf before she was fully out of site.

'You're an idiot,' I turned at the voice. It was Agua, she was sitting at one of the benches. 'Now I have to go deal with that.'

'Our relationship was a lie,' I stated. 'A ruse to get closer to my father.'

'That is not true,' Agua seemed shocked by my comment. 'She might have used it yesterday, but she never had any intentions of doing so.' She glanced me over. 'And you know that, otherwise you wouldn't be so worried about her.'

'I'm not worried about her. She can obviously take care of herself.'

'I can sense it all over you,' she told me. 'You reek of anxiety.'

'I don't know what to do?' I admitted.

'Trust her. Trust us,' she said. 'We're the only thing keeping you alive.'

'How can I trust you?' I asked. 'Everything I've been told was a lie.'

'The rest of us yes,' she agreed. 'We keep ourselves fairly invisible, but Rya has tried her best to be as honest as possible, especially with you. She hated lying to you.' She slipped off the bench. 'Come with me.'

'Why?' My voice was guarded.

'Just trust me,' she said. Despite the events of the last twenty-four hours, I did.

RYA GARCIA

'What is he doing here?' We were barely thirty minutes from shifting.

'I asked her the exact same thing,' Toby said flatly. 'She wouldn't explain herself.'

'You want him to trust us?' Agua asked incredulously. 'Do you want him to keep the secret?' Our silence was answer enough.

'But this?' I asked. 'It isn't exactly the best place to start.'

'Did you think we would be happy about this?' Toby demanded, I saw him glance at Zac.

'There's nothing we can do about it now.' I got to my feet. If I didn't start moving I was going to go crazy. I tucked my hands under my arms. 'Where's the kid?' I asked Agua, she had been watching me pace.

'She's here somewhere,' Agua responded.

'I hate dark moons,' Toby growled getting to his feet. He started pacing on the other side of the room.

'Should we take you down then?' Agua asked.

'We've still got like twenty minutes,' I reminded her.

'You guys are making me edgy.' I hadn't realised I'd started pacing again.

I took a deep breath, trying my best to keep calm. Zac seemed to be curious. I suppose that was better than being afraid of me. 'Where are you kid?' I said, my voice a little louder than before.

'I'm here.' She appeared around the wall from the direction of the bedrooms. 'Does it always feel like this?' she asked. She looked like she was trying to hold herself together.

'It doesn't get much easier,' I admitted. I blinked away my flashing eyes. The first signs that it was almost time. 'Now we should go,' I stated as the other two experienced something similar.

They couldn't blink it away like I did. Toby's eyes burned through his contacts and started flickering in the growing darkness along with Maya's. Agua didn't hesitate, she went to the bookshelf in the corner.

She pressed the button hidden on the corner of the middle shelf. After a moment, the entire bookshelf shifted to the side, as if on wheels. I ignored Zac's shocked expression and led the way down the two flights of stairs.

The heavy metal door at the entrance stood open. I passed it without a second thought and walked into the cage beyond. Toby was a step behind me. It was only Maya that hesitated. Her eyes were now solidly glowing. A quick glance at Toby told me he was the same.

After Maya forced herself to enter Agua closed the door and locked it. She then laid her hand on the lock and whispered a word in Latin. I wasn't sure what she said. Lock and hand both glowed, sealing shut for the night. The spell wouldn't wear off until Agua wanted it to.

I leaned against the far wall. The other two didn't go so far, they sat down against the two remaining walls. I tried not to wince as the first tremor struck me. My breath caught in my chest. I forced myself to stay upright.

The others were already changing. They were hunched over, clutching themselves, trying to block out the pain they were feeling. Toby let out a grunt as his spine curled. He was getting better at this. Maybe it was the idea of a human audience.

I unclenched my fists when I felt my claws dig into my palms. I took several deep breaths and I crouched low. I could feel the fangs in my mouth with my tongue. Four large canines pushing their way out of my mouth.

I couldn't stop the gasp as my bones started to crack and reshape themselves. I sealed my mouth shut and breathed heavily through my nose. My transformation was faster than theirs, so while they started turning first, I was the first to finish.

I shook out my fur, the shreds of my clothes falling to the ground below me. When I felt the familiar pressure on my mind I handed over the reins and I was thrown into the abyss.

AGUA FRAY

This was something I had seen many times before.
Toby was still half human, Rya's wolf was already
pacing around the small space, occasionally staring
out impatiently at us. 'It looks different for each of
them,' Zac observed in a voice almost too low to
hear.

'Because they fight it, Rya doesn't,' I told him.
'Maya is new to this, as you heard last night. She
would have been pushing against it, it takes longer
and it hurts more.'

'What about him?' He was looking at the
hunched over Toby, his snout was currently
pushing out.

'He has a little more experience but not so much
that he doesn't naturally try to fight it.' I looked at
the pacing white wolf. 'Rya just lets it all go. She
might as well give up control of her body. That
makes her transformation faster and less painful.'

'How long has she been this way?' he asked me.
He was also watching the progress of the wolf.

'She's been able to transform for about six

years,' I responded. 'For three of those she was learning how to control it.'

'But he's fine and you said he's only been doing this a few months.'

'Rya's not just a werewolf,' I explained. 'She's one of the strongest ever born. A part of that has to do with her bloodline, another part is because of what happened the first night she turned.'

'What happened?' I should have expected that one.

'Not for me to tell you,' I said. 'She's had a hard six years.'

They were all fully wolf now. Rya's wolf had stopped pacing and seemed to be waiting for Toby to get to his feet. Maya sat warily in the corner, trying not to be noticed by the other wolves. I could have laughed when Toby pounced at Rya. The two started wrestling playfully.

'Come on,' I told the human next to me. 'They're going to be like this for hours; there's no point waiting down here.'

The three wolves turned to look as we moved; I could feel their stares on my back as I led Zac out of the room. I pulled shut the metal door and blocked their sight. Making sure it was locked before leading Zac back upstairs.

Since coming down the bookcase had closed itself. The back of it was also plated with metal. It had a small round button on the back that would open it. I closed the bookcase behind us after Zac followed me out.

'What do we do now?' he asked.

'Eat, talk and sleep,' I told him. 'I can't go anywhere until they wake up.'

RYA GARCIA

I woke up to the sound of the metal door opening. My head was resting on Toby's bare chest and my body was curled up in such a way that I had to be part canine. Toby drew in a deep breath beneath me, right before he stretched.

I stretched my own body as Agua unlocked the gate. I rubbed my eyes with the heels of my hands and the world came into focus. I flinched when Agua threw something at me. It took me until just before the bundle reached me to realise what it was; I caught the clothes. She threw more clothes to Toby and Maya.

While I had woken up next to Toby, Maya couldn't have been further away. Her wolf hadn't been accepted by ours then. Just enough to leave her alone. I pulled my shirt over my head, once I was on my feet I pulled on my shorts. Then I gathered the scraps of clothing strewn about the concrete floor. I hated the morning after more than the day of the dark moon. It felt like I had a tonne of weight sitting on my shoulders. I forced myself to walk upstairs after Agua who had already disappeared.

I almost collapsed onto the stool at the bench. Agua was already cooking food. I looked into the pan, steak and bacon. She knew how to make it a little better. I put my head in my hands, I could barely focus, when Agua put the crispy bacon and partially cooked steak in front of me.

'No, Toby,' I winced at Agua's loud voice. 'Food first.' It always amused me how she treated us like kids the day after the dark moon.

I rubbed my eyes again and forced myself to eat. I

completely ignored the utensils next to the plate. 'Rya, at least try to be human,' Agua said, directing the same voice on me. 'We have a guest.'

'I'm going to need a shower and several hours of sleep before I resemble anything close to human,' I reminded her. To be honest I hadn't noticed Zac sitting at the table across the room. Apparently Zac had stayed the night. Did this mean he was okay with all this? What had Agua been telling him.

Toby and Maya slumped into the chairs on either side of me. Agua gave them the same food as I had in front of me. I pushed away my empty plate when I was done eating. 'I'm going to bed.' I announced, forcing myself to my feet.

After a long shower of sitting in the bottom and let the hot water run over me, I crawled on my bed and slumped onto the cloud of softness. It felt too soft. I had a brief recollection of Toby heading past me to the shower. I even heard the other shower start up.

I wasn't expecting Maya to crawl onto the bed after Toby. I didn't blame her, I didn't know how she would be feeling right now. With the three of us curled together on the bed I drifted into a deep sleep.

ZAC HALL

'So, what's going on with you and Rya?' Dylan asked as we changed for the game.

'Nothing,' I answered. He didn't believe me. 'Just a disagreement.'

'That girl looked pretty pissed yesterday,' Sean half

shouted from across the room. 'I suggest apologising and moving on.'

'It's not that simple,' I admitted.

They looked worried now. 'What happened?' The others were listening but they were staying out of it. I was closer to these two then the others.

'Not something I can talk about.' Agua had managed to convince me to stay quiet, for now at least.

'Is she going to be here tonight?' Dylan asked.

'I don't know,' I stated getting to my feet. 'Let's just go warm up. I really don't want to think about it right now.'

Sean and I spent the next hour putting the team through several warm up drills. By the time the other team arrived we were ready to go.

I pushed my shin guards under my knee-high socks, red, for the team colours. Wolfridge Wolves. When we were only ten minutes from kick-off coach gave us the normal play-by-play outlook. Nobody bothered listening to this, all we did was keep formation, the rest would change in the middle of play.

I was so uninterested in this game that I was scanning the crowd. I was a little shocked to see Rya sitting there beside Agua and Toby's family. I was glad she was here. God, I was confused. Someone tell me what to do.

RYA GARCIA

The game was great. They won. Which meant they were in the finals next week. Second time in a row. That put our team in the finals next week against the Wolfridge Preparatory Academy. The only other high school in Wolfridge.

Broken up into two schools, state and private. The Academy had a boarding facility and also included elementary school. Our school, the state high school, was down the road from Wolfridge Elementary. The boarding school was used mostly by rich kids and farmers. It was for parents that either didn't have time for their kids, or no longer had the ability to teach them from home.

They were a tough team to beat having taken the finals from us last year. And all those players were counting on the scouts from nearby colleges. Nearby meaning not in town. As far as I remembered two colleges were sending people to this district final. NYU and the college two towns over. Most of the boys wouldn't be graduating until next year, but they could hope for early admission scholarships. I knew that's what Zac was hoping for.

As the other team got back into cars and a team bus the locals started to disperse, taking the younger kids with them. Some of the teenagers went with them, the ones that didn't really like the scene that followed a win. That usually involved dinner at the local teen bar before loud music at the park across the road.

I usually went with Zac, but I didn't go to his side after the game like I usually did. Instead I stayed with Toby and Agua. We shared a bowl of chips and headed out to the park. There was a playground off to one side for the little kids, however right now it sported about a dozen 15 to 17-year-olds.

The three of us sat in a small circle near the lake. The good thing about this town was that, the teenagers partied every other week, but there was never any alcohol involved. The beauty of a small town. All alcohol was consumed within houses with parent permission. Not that alcohol affected werewolves anyway, our metabolism was too fast.

'You're quiet,' Agua commented, breaking through my thoughts.

'I'm just really hoping Zac won't tell anybody about me.'

'If he does, he'll deal with me.' Toby's voice was spiteful. He was looking across the crowd at Zac.

'Thanks, but no thanks,' I said. 'I'd rather he keeps his head.'

'Don't forget he knows about us too.'

Agua spoke up. 'I don't think he will tell,' She put in. 'I spoke to him last night. He's more confused than anything.'

I sighed. I hated feeling this worried. I hadn't been with him long enough to prejudge his reaction. Honestly, I thought that if I did tell him, he would be fine with it. He found out too soon. Not long enough to understand.

I looked up, my eyes met Zac's for a moment before I broke the stare. I got to my feet. 'Where are you going?' Toby asked me.

'To clear my head,' I answered walking towards the forest. It was probably foolish to walk that way with people on the lookout for Hall's werewolf, but then, people always went into the forest on these nights, if you get what I mean.

I was maybe 100 metres in before I heard running feet behind me. I turned to see Zac coming after me.

'What do you want?' I asked, a little more abrupt then I was expecting.

I regretted my tone when I sensed his hurt. 'I'm trying to understand all of this,' he said. 'I am, but it's not easy to do that.'

'Because of your loyalty to your father,' I stated.

'We're not dogs,' he retorted.

'Canines had nothing to do with my comment. Even humans can be loyal.' I stared challengingly into his eyes. 'I don't know why I fooled myself into thinking this would work. Your father has made it his goal to catch and study werewolves.'

'That doesn't mean I'll help him.'

'I can't keep looking over my shoulder every time you don't like how I live.' I took a breath. 'It would be easier if I left now, before everyone else finds out. Your father is too close. Closer than he's ever been. It's better for the pack to migrate,' I sighed.

I turned around. 'Erik,' I said with clenched teeth. 'What are you doing this close to town?' He was in human form for once. His skin was dirty, his clothes ripped and worn with messy black hair on the top of his head.

'It's my territory, I can do what I want.'

'It's not your territory,' I stated. 'You stole it.' I glanced back at Zac. 'Go back to the park.'

He didn't need to be told twice. He turned on his heel and walked at a fast pace towards the bright lights. 'You doubt him?' Erik asked me.

'Sure,' I said. 'I fear for the packs safety.'

'And yet he still lives.'

'I won't kill a human,' I told him. 'Especially one I care about.'

'I'll do it for you then.' He smirked in the direction Zac had gone.

I stepped in front of him. 'No, you won't.'

He raised questioning eyebrows. 'It sounded like you just gave me an order.'

'You're not my alpha,' I returned. 'I don't answer to you.'

He gave me a smirk before rushing forward. I expected him to come at me, but instead he flew past me in blur of skin, cloth and fur. It took me a moment to register what he was doing. As soon as I did I took off after him, shedding my own human skin as I rushed to catch up.

He was over the tree line before I caught up. He was just about to leap onto Zac who had his back turned, but he heard us just in time to dive out of the way. I collided with Erik before he had the chance. I knocked Erik to the ground. He twisted as he fell reaching with his jaw to grab me.

He missed. I managed to close my jaw on his canine shoulder. A growl rumbled in his throat as he wrestled to gain the upper hand. It didn't take him long, and when it did start to happen I broke away, circling around to face him again. I lowered my head, a growl echoing in my throat.

Blood dripped from his wounded shoulder even as I started tasting it in my mouth. We both moved at the same time. I jumped before we collided. I grabbed the fur of his neck as I sailed over him, my weight pulled him to the ground beneath me.

He rolled before I could close my jaw over his throat. Instead it audibly clacked shut. He lurched towards me, knocking me over until he stood over me. I curled my hind legs into my body. Before he could snap his jaw shut I kicked out. He was flung backwards. I rolled easily to my feet.

He was still laying on the ground when I looked over at him. He stared at me. I only lowered my head and growled threateningly. He didn't seem to know how to react to me. I was stopping him at every turn.

He lurched suddenly to his feet and bolted towards me in the same moment I lurched forward. His gaze had turned murderous. This fight was just beginning. He grabbed my foreleg at the same moment I gripped his neck in my jaw.

I pushed down on him as he closed teeth around bone. I couldn't stop my whimper. However, I forced myself to hold onto his throat. He rolled, and I could taste his blood flowing into my mouth, gagging me.

Instead of rolling he slammed us both into the ground. I was on my back, still gripping his neck. I felt his claws rest on my chest a moment later. I couldn't remember letting go, all I felt was the sting of deep open wounds from chest to stomach.

I barely moved before his jaw snapped shut, where my exposed throat had just been. I staggered to my feet, with a broken leg and my long wounds I was struggling. Still I refused to submit.

When Erik looked like he was about to run for me I was surprised when he dove in another direction, a moment later I saw why. A tranquiliser was sticking out of the ground where he had just been. I dodged a second one directed at me by rolling to the side.

Big mistake. I had overestimated my remaining

strength. I pushed myself up as Erik dove towards me, he was ignoring the animal control interference. I wasn't fast enough to get out of his way. It was only him dodging another dart that saved me.

Erik turned towards the humans, a growl in his throat as he started towards them. I used my remaining strength to get in his way. Honestly, standing was painful, but I didn't back down. The growl I gave him was threatening and dominant.

I didn't have the strength to fight him off. I had lost too much blood by this time and it was getting more difficult to stay conscious. He attacked me and I once again ended up beneath his paws. I glared up at him. *'You may be stronger, but I will never submit to you,'* I growled.

He was just about to attack me when the humans shot more darts. It missed him, but I wasn't fast enough to move, as injured as I was. The needle sank into my hind leg. *'I'll deal with you later,'* Erik growled. Without another word, he bolted back into the forest.

I forced myself to my feet, but before I could take more than a step another dart hit me, this time I felt the liquid seep through my body. I shook my head to clear it as I moved towards the forest. I should have known it was fruitless, within seconds the drugs pulled me under and I was thrown into darkness.

AGUA FRAY

I had to stop Toby from rushing forward. When Rya collapsed I was tempted to go myself. Then she became human. There was a mixture of shock and an emotion I couldn't pick going around the crowd of teenagers.

Blood coated her body. I knew that the blood on her face was Erik's. She had done really well, and that had caught him off guard. It wasn't long before I heard the sirens in the distance, announcing the arrival of police and I think an ambulance.

Toby almost yanked me forward when Hall arrived on the scene. 'No, Toby,' I said, using some of my own strength to hold him in place. 'If you go, they'll find out about you too.'

'I don't care,' He growled. 'This is Rya.'

'She wouldn't want us to risk everybody's lives for hers,' I told him, surprised by the reason in my own voice. 'We go away, we come up with a plan, then we go in. We have to be smart about it.'

I was glad we were at the back of the crowd, it was stopping them from seeing what was going on between us. He stopped struggling. I could have sighed as my grip relaxed. 'We'll call Colby and Seth and everybody else. Then we come up with a plan.'

I could see Zac watching us from where he sat, he seemed to have gotten over whatever shock he had been experiencing from the attack. I shook my head slightly telling him not to do anything. I think he understood. Because he didn't protest as his father put Rya into the back of his van.

RYA GARCIA

I rammed myself against the door. It moved but it didn't buckle. I stepped back before rushing forward again. My shoulder was sore now. I had woken up in this room. I had no idea how long I had been out. Long enough for my wounds to heal I suppose.

I stepped back again. My breath was coming in sharp gasps. The trapped feeling was slowly breaking through my self-control. The only kind thing they'd done for me since being shoved in this room was that they'd left some clothes for me.

I ran my hands stressfully through my hair as I continued to step backwards. I bumped into the wall behind me and slid to the floor. I leaned my head back, eyes closed as I focused on staying human. Not an easy thing to do in such a small room.

Then I heard the door open. It was so unexpected. Only open for the briefest of moments as a girl was thrown inside with me. 'Maya.' I was at her side in seconds. The door closed just as quickly.

Maya flinched at my touch, rolling away from me as her skin started to melt. 'Maya, it's okay,' I said to her. I could see her reining it in, but most young werewolves couldn't handle being trapped.

She had her head on her knee as her skin rippled with grey fur. I gently rested my hand on her shoulder. It was a soothing touch. 'Remember what I taught you.' My voice was soft as she leaned into the touch.

I reached my mind out to surround hers. I knew that she would sense my own anxiety, but my goal was to keep her under control. She slowed her breathing, taking long, deep breaths as my calm enveloped her.

I relaxed when her skin stopped rippling. 'How do you do this?' she asked, almost collapsing into a sitting position.

Sometimes I didn't even know. 'A lot of practice,' I answered.

'You get tossed in rooms by humans often?'

I smirked despite the situation. 'No, this is a first for me,' I admitted. 'But I have been in a lot worse situations than this.' Getting locked in Erik's hole of a basement for one. 'How'd they get you?'

'I think they came crashing into the house,' she said. She seemed like she was trying to clear it. 'I don't know it's all foggy.'

'They must have gone in just after they took me,' I considered. 'Otherwise you would have been taken somewhere safe.'

'What happened to you?' she asked me in a small voice. 'Aren't you supposed to be the stealthy one?'

'There's no way to be stealthy when Erik decides to do something crazy.' She looked curious. 'He went after Zac.' I explained.

'That's the guy from the other night, right?'

I nodded. 'Erik didn't trust him enough to let him live with our secret.'

'Does he trust anyone?'

I shrugged. 'Not for a very long time.' I looked down at her. 'I think he's starting to really lose it now,' I stated. 'Usually he would have waited to take out the threat. Then it would be up to us to clean up his mess.'

Maya looked around the empty room. There was a camera in each corner watching, and probably listening to everything we said. 'So how are we getting out of here?'

'The door is pretty solid,' I admitted. 'There's no point going for walls because they're lined with cement. We're probably underground. I can't break us out without things getting bloody on the other side.' I had given her the low down on my family after the dark moon, which included the strength of my own wolf.

'So then what?'

'We wait them out,' I told her. 'Eventually they'll come to us.'

AGUA FRAY

'Why aren't we doing anything?' Toby demanded in a hushed whisper.

'The pack told us not to,' I reminded him.

'And when has that stopped us before.'

'Keep your voice down,' I warned. We were sitting

in the middle of the school cafeteria. The whole town took Rya's werewolf status strangely. Some didn't seem to believe it, more so the adults that weren't there, even though three quarters of the high school had seen a wolf turn into Rya Garcia.

Zac hadn't been seen since that night, neither had Alec for that matter. 'I can't just sit here and do nothing.' He got to his feet.

'What are you going to do?' I asked. 'You don't even know where she's being kept.'

'I don't care,' he said. 'I'll tear the place apart if I have to.'

'You won't have to.' I was shocked to hear Zac's voice.

'Father let you off the leash, did he?' Toby sneered.

Zac's mouth twitched like he had thought better of responding. 'If you don't want to find out where my father is keeping her, then I'll leave.'

'No,' I said before Toby could say something stupid. 'What do you have?' I asked.

'She's being kept in an underground cell at the lab. It's about three floors below ground level.' He looked at Toby. 'I'm guessing you can get the schematics.'

Toby released a short laugh as he opened his laptop. 'Please,' He scoffed. 'I wouldn't be a Davis if I couldn't get a few building schematics.'

'Not if these ones are government classified.'

'And I'm not quite up to DOD hacking yet,' he sighed.

'What about the builders?' I asked suddenly.

Toby grinned as he started typing. 'Going to the source,' he muttered. 'Got it,' he announced. 'It's a big time builder that works out of New York, they do most of the government's work. Give me a moment to jump on their server. If they built that entire building they'll have floor plans.'

As promised a few moments later Toby had the drawings on his screen. 'Okay.' Zac stepped forward, then stepped to the side when Toby glared at him. 'She's being held in this room here, the one next to it is surveillance for the cameras in each corner.'

'Is Maya with her?' Toby asked. She was gone by the time we got to the house the other night, and the house had been ransacked.

'Yes,' Zac answered.

'What about Erik?' Toby was looking at me. 'If we get Rya out then he'll kill her.'

'There are places she can go to stay away from Erik,' I assured him.

'Do you really think he'll kill her?' Zac asked.

'The other night's fight was different,' I told him. 'If they hadn't been interrupted one of them would be dead now.'

'Then what do we do?'

'You do nothing,' Toby's voice was serious.

'I want to help. It's my fault she's in there.'

'It sure is,' Toby stated.

'You'll just slow us down,' I told him. 'Hopefully we can get in and out without being seen.'

'Doubtful,' Zac stated. 'Security is pretty tight down there.'

I sensed Toby's suspicion as he glared up at Zac. 'How do we know this isn't a trap?'

'I'm trying to help.'

'That's not enough for me,' Toby said. 'You disappear with your father for three days and suddenly reappear with information.'

'I've been getting myself access. My father wasn't exactly willing to let me in after Rya was talking to Maya about me knowing everything.'

'You know nothing,' Toby snarled. 'You might know the truth but you know nothing about us. Any of us.'

'This is getting us nowhere,' I said turning to Toby. 'As much as you hate it, we're going to have to trust him.'

Toby stood up so that he was taller then Zac. 'If this is a trap, I will kill you myself. I don't care about the law.'

He was serious too. I could sense it. I think Zac could too. You had to admire his strength. Most humans would have cowered under a gaze like that from a werewolf. 'There is still the problem of you two getting in without being seen.'

I raised an eyebrow slightly. He still didn't really know what I was. 'That's where I come in.'

RYA GARCIA

I was right. When the door did finally open we were sitting in the corner, Maya was curled up with her head on my lap and I was leaning against the wall, dozing to pass the time. Who knew if I would need the energy later.

Maya sat blot up right the moment the door slid to the side. It was Hall, of course. Maya growled audibly. After being trapped in this room for hours, her wolf was close to the surface. I put a hand on her shoulder. She stopped growling as my touch settled her.

I got to my feet and stood in front of the younger werewolf. 'What do you want?' I asked him, my arms were crossed.

'That depends on what you want?' he responded.

'I want to go home and I want to be left alone,' I stated. 'I have enough going on in my life without having to worry about you.'

'Tell me what I want to know and you can go.'

I could have laughed. 'I highly doubt that, because I'm not telling you anything.'

'Which is why I have him,' Alec said as the door opened again. A man stepped through the open door and it quickly closed again. 'He's one of the government's best operatives. He specialises in getting criminals to talk.'

'What's he going to do?' I asked. 'I can tell you that there isn't one thing that he can do to me that is worse than what I've already been through.'

'You know, the good thing about you not being human is that I don't have to worry about human rights,' the man said in a deep voice. He pulled the gun out of its holster in a split second. It took me only a moment to notice where he pointed it.

I stepped in the same second that he shot. My leg buckled as the metal pierced my leg. I looked up at the human. 'You're going to shoot a child?' I growled. I held my hand to the wound, stopping excessive loss of blood.

I took a deep breath as my wolf rose to the surface. I felt my eyes flash. I took another breath as I blinked them away. Maya stepped forward, a growl in her throat. 'No,' I said, grabbing her arm. 'It's a test.'

'Well done,' the man said as Maya stepped back again. 'You're smarter than you look.'

'Not all werewolves have my level of control,' I stated. I sucked in a breath and reached into the wound. The bullet hadn't gone all the way through. Instead it had gotten itself caught between bone and muscle.

When my fingers finally reached the piece of metal I carefully dislodged it and pulled it out. It clattered to the floor beside me. My finger and thumb were clawed, it was the only way I could pull it out without doing more damage. I curled my fist and the two claws disappeared.

'How are you not in pain?' Alec asked.

I glared at him. 'I've been shot before,' I told him. 'It's not exactly a new feeling.'

The government man pulled something out of his pocket. 'Then let's try something different.' It snapped out as he flicked it, kind of like one of those toy lightsabers, but without the light. He struck out at Maya. The girl crumpled, screaming in pain.

An intake of breath exposed the hot scent of electricity. 'Stop it!!' I shouted. He stopped and Maya collapsed as the remaining electricity rushed through her body.

I was already beside her and I could already sense her wolf rippling beneath her skin. I touched my hand to her cheek. 'Maya.' My voice was soft.

She was curled into a ball, holding herself as her wolf fought for freedom. It happened pretty quickly after that. There was no way she could withstand her wolf in this situation. All I could do was hold her down as she writhed in pain. It was hurting her so much that she couldn't make a sound. I knew, I'd been there before.

When the grey wolf looked up at me I couldn't see Maya behind those eyes. For now, she was gone. 'It's okay,' I told the wolf, looking deeply into her eyes.

Even her wolf recognised me as more dominant then she was. She lowered her gaze and whined, I was meant to protect her. 'It's okay,' I repeated. 'You're safe with me. Okay. You're safe.'

I held my hand out over the wolf's muzzle, inviting it. After a moment, the wolf leaned into the palm of my right hand. I took a deep breath and brushed my hand down the side of her head. Before the wolf realised what I was doing, I had already dug my fingers into the pressure point below her ear. In an instant the wolf collapsed, completely unconscious.

I felt the tension in the room disappear slightly. I looked up at the two humans. 'Are you trying to get yourselves killed?'

TOBY DAVIS

When we arrived at the outskirts of the lab, Agua stopped me. 'Ready?' she asked seriously. I wasn't too sure. 'You don't have to go in,' she said. 'I can do this on my own.'

'You're not going in alone,' my voice was firm. 'Are you even sure that you can do this?'

'We'll soon find out.'

Why didn't I like the sound of that? I sighed. I stooped down to my bag and grabbed out one of our family hacking devices. It was a homemade contraption designed to unlock any electronic security system, including government ones.

Agua put a hand on my shoulder. 'Caecus.' I heard her mutter.

Rya might be used to the magic this witch cast on her but I wasn't. I had never been the one to receive the flow of energy. I stopped myself from squirming as my body went numb. Then my skin felt like it was burning, like when I had gotten too close to the pack fire when we were kids.

Then it was gone. I felt back to normal. I looked down at my body. It was still there. 'Did it work?' I asked her.

'Yes,' she said. 'Humans can't see us. I don't need to take it to supernaturals too.' She paused for a moment. 'Let's go.'

We ran all the way to the laboratory. It was easy to take the front gate, it stood wide open; only one guard was watching everybody enter. It was almost amusing when he didn't see us run past. We reached the door. It was closed.

I held the hack device over the keypad next to the door. Numbers flittered across the screen until it gave the system the right code. The door clicked open and we slipped inside through the smallest gap possible.

'Remember they can hear and feel us,' Agua whispered behind me. 'And if they touch you the spell will be removed.'

'I know,' I said as we reached another coded door in our way. This place was like Fort Knox, which I hadn't been to by the way. I'd only looked at plans and studied the security systems.

'Come on Toby,' Agua said impatiently. We were entering the underground level.

'It takes a while if it hasn't come across the program before,' I told her. Finally the door clicked open. I grinned. 'We got the program.' The door led to stairs going downwards. Underground like the Hall kid said. We had to stop and press ourselves against the wall as two humans came up the narrow steps.

I almost gaped when we reach the bottom. I'd seen the room on the schematics but this was massive. 'Werewolf central,' I stated quietly.

Things on werewolves covered every wall, nook and cranny. 'Come on,' Agua whispered, pulling me towards the room where Rya was apparently being held.

I looked around at the various workbenches. People in lab coats were everywhere. This was what werewolves feared would happen if they were ever discovered. This was going to be bad.

We came to the right door. At least we hope so. It was locked, of course. I put the hacking device against the keypad and it did its thing. When the door clicked open we waited. A moment later somebody opened it. We quickly ducked inside.

'Who was it?' said another voice. Another man sitting in the corner.

'Nobody,' the man responded. He closed the door and turn back around.

I slipped behind him intending to be able to see the screens. It was just my luck that he stepped back. I swore as the magic slipped off my skin the moment he touched me. 'Who the hell are you?'

'Toby,' Agua said. 'Open the door.'

I easily dodged the human and ran to the door. I could see what was happening in the screens. I practically threw myself across the room before anybody could touch me.

Without thinking I pressed my hacker to the system that would open the door. This one used a swipe card. Easy. It only took a moment before the door clicked open. Before I even touched it, it blew open and Agua stalked into the room ahead of me.

I wasn't expecting the gun that was pointed at me. I stopped myself from stepping away from the firearm, it wouldn't help in this small space anyway. 'Don't shoot him.' Rya was crouched next to unconscious Maya. Blood coated Rya's leg, anger rose within me, how dare they hurt her.

'Who are you?' The man with the gun asked.

I didn't answer, but Hall did. 'It's one of her friends,' he stated. 'They must be werewolves too.'

'You're despicable,' I was surprised by the growl in Agua's voice. 'You find out that werewolves actually do exist and the first thing you do is torture them for information.'

'She wasn't talking.'

'Did it get you anywhere?' she demanded.

'I can get information out you two,' he pulled the trigger.

The bullet shot out of the barrel, it never met its

target. 'That is so cool.' I was staring at the bullet frozen in the air before Agua. After a moment it dropped to the ground.

Agua hadn't been the only one doing something. Rya, moving slower than the bullet had, dived onto the man, knocking him to the ground. He rolled over in an instant and shot again. I only heard her growl of pain as the bullet went straight through her body.

'Hey, trigger happy,' Agua said. 'Gimme your gun.' She held her hand out and the handgun flew out of his hand as Rya staggered off the human.

She was hunched over, hand over the wound on her stomach. I could also see the blood on her back from the exit wound. She gasped as her wolf, at least I assumed it was her wolf, forced her to the ground.

She was taking deep heavy breaths as she fought for control. She growled in pain when her arm snapped, her body rippling as the wolf pushed. I almost expected her to lose control, but I should know better by now.

The room was filled with Rya's breathing, the slightest rumble of a growl echoing within her throat. I saw her wince as her arm popped back into a human position. A few deep breaths later she seemed to collapse with exhaustion.

She looked sideways at Agua. 'Get us out of here.' She sounded out of breath. She gulped. 'I don't think I can take another bullet.'

Before Agua said anything, I walked over and picked up the still unconscious Maya. 'You think we're just going to let you walk out of here?' Hall questioned.

'I don't think we're giving you a choice,' Rya said, pushing herself to her feet. She was glaring at the human. She couldn't seem to be able to hide her exhaustion. 'I think I'd rather talk to you on the other side when I haven't just been shot. Twice.'

Agua put a hand on both our shoulders, this time she didn't use a word. All I felt was the magic rush over me. Then it felt like... I didn't even know how to describe it. Maybe the closest I could get was getting sucked into a black hole. One moment we were standing in the bright white cell and the next we were thrown into darkness.

AGUA FRAY

I collapsed onto my bed completely exhausted. I had never used so much magic before. I had just started to drift off when my bedroom door opened. 'Where have you been?' I winced. I hadn't seen my mother in days.

'Around,' I responded. My mother didn't know what I was.

'You haven't been home in days.'

Yes I have, just when she hasn't seen me. 'Mum you work a lot, it's not uncommon to not see each other.'

'You were off with Rya weren't you?'

'Actually no,' I responded. 'In case you haven't noticed she's locked up at Alec Hall's lab.'

I sat up when she sat down on my bed. 'You knew what she was didn't you?'

For a split second I considered lying. But then I'm sure Hall would expose me and Toby soon enough. 'Yes, I did.'

'You didn't tell anybody?'

'I wasn't able to,' I told her truthfully. 'And I was protecting her.'

'How long have you known?' she asked.

'Since Ry became a werewolf.' I looked her in the eyes. 'She's not dangerous. The other one, the black wolf is, but Ry isn't.' God, I sounded like a desperate kid trying to keep its pet.

I heard the front door open and close. I didn't think much of it. It was probably Dad. 'I wish you could have told me,' my mother said.

'I'm sorry,' I said. 'But it was important to keep you out of everything.'

'There you are,' a voice said when a man appeared at the door.

I didn't look much like my mother, she had blonde hair, fair skin and blue eyes; the complete opposite to my tanned skin, dark brown hair and brown eyes. But stand me next to my father and there was no denying our relation. Of course it was more than just looks that we shared.

Like the Garcia family, the Fray family had a long history of magical blood. The magic passed down to the first-born child, me. If there was a second child and the first born died, the powers were passed onto the next sibling.

My father's case was different. He had a twin sister that we didn't see very often. Like my father she also had magical abilities, which meant that her child, my cousin, would also have magical abilities. But I'd never met my two cousins. They lived on the other side of the country in a small town inhabited by skinwalkers my aunt assisted them when required. It was kind of like we did for the werewolf pack.

For the last two years, my father had teaching me

how to use my powers. We had only just been starting to move onto more powerful magic like teleporting. I was actually surprised that I managed to carry all three of us without any complications.

'Don't all talk at once,' my father said, looking between us.

He gave me a look. The, "we need to talk" look.

'We were just talking about Rya,' my mother admitted.

Another look. 'Really?'

'Did you know about her being a werewolf, because you don't seem surprised about this either?'

He looked at me. A question. My father probably should have told my mother what we were years ago. I shrugged, I didn't care, because of me we were going to be found out anyway. My father looked at his wife's uncertain face. 'I knew about her,' he admitted.

RYA GARCIA

I was sitting on the edge of the bed when Maya woke up. Her head kind of lolled to the side, before she caught it. Her eyes opened then blinked several times, slowly taking in the scene before her. She sat up.

'It's okay,' I said pushing her back down. 'We're okay.'

She looked at me, relaxing, but she didn't lay back down. 'Where are we?' she asked.

'At the bunker,' I responded. 'It's the safest place for us be until we work out what to do.'

'What are we going to do?' She sounded exhausted.

'I don't know,' I admitted. 'The others are coming here so we can discuss our options.'

'This is all my fault.' Her voice was watery, as her eyes brimmed with moisture. 'If I hadn't have come here they wouldn't know about you.'

'Maybe. Maybe not.' I hated these situations, I never knew what to do without it feeling awkward. 'We've had issues around here for years, and it was only a matter of time before Hall found one of us. We've been here too long.'

'I'm sorry.'

I don't even really know how it happened, but she was in my arms, sobbing into my shirt. I didn't know what to do. Trying to console her seemed petty and irrelevant at this point. So I just held her as she sobbed uncontrollably in my arms.

When she did finally stop I spoke to her; I'd had a little bit of time to think about what I would say. 'We're going to find out a way to get through this,' I promised. 'We might be able to cut a deal.'

She sniffed as she pulled away. 'I didn't mean to get all sooky on you.' She was looking down, ashamed of herself.

I lifted her chin up so she looked me in the eyes. 'We all go over that edge at some point.' I gave her a small smile as I wiped the tears off her cheek.

She leaned into my touch, taking the small amount of comfort it gave her. 'I think you should stay down here for the meeting,' I told her. 'You're in no condition to sit in.'

'But...'

'I want you to rest,' I told her. 'You need your sleep.

I'll be doing the same thing after the meeting.'

'You'll tell me what happens?'

'In the morning.'

'Promise?'

'Promise.' And with that she laid back on the pillows, rolled over and instantly fell asleep.

I silently slid off the bed and walked out of the room. Toby was leaning against the wall outside her room. 'How is she?' he asked.

'She blames herself,' I told him. 'She's a mess.'

'What about you?'

'I'll heal.' I walked past him. I was still limping slightly.

'That's not what I meant and you know it.'

'Well, it's the only answer you're getting.'

I went into my own temporary room across the hall. Toby followed me.

'Rya?' he said as I pulled my shirt over my head. I ignored Toby as I pulled a new one out of the hastily packed bag. 'Rya!'

'What Toby?' I snapped. 'What do you want me to say to you? I wasn't humiliated by Erik in front of a group humans we go to school with. I didn't just spend three days trapped in a small room in a scientist's laboratory being observed before they tried to torture me.' I turned on him. 'I was fine with that because I would have gotten myself out of it.' He lowered his gaze. 'You disobeyed a direct order from your dominants. They knew what was at stake, I knew what was at stake and I would have preferred being locked up to exposing everyone else.' My voice was elevated now. 'You've exposed your family and

Agua's. Now we have to come up with a way to clean up the mess you've made worse.'

'I was trying to help.'

'You didn't think about the consequences.' He was visibly cowering now. He knew he was in trouble. 'Just go upstairs.' I pulled the new shirt over my head. He was gone before my head was through the hole.

When I did make it upstairs everyone was there. 'Nice of you to join us Rya,' Erik stated.

8

I ducked out early the next morning to hunt. Toby and Agua had decided to go to school, not knowing if Alec had revealed them. They couldn't stand sitting around doing nothing either. Besides, we needed to know what was happening.

When I flew out of the bunker that morning it was on four legs. I didn't have to worry about humans seeing me out here. It was rare for them to come this far into the forest without Erik killing them. I couldn't believe how good it felt to stretch my legs as I ran to the hunting grounds.

It didn't take me long to find a grazing herd of deer, I moved so I was down wind where they wouldn't be able to smell me coming. I chose my target and walked swiftly and silently on my toes, a technique I picked up from the coyotes.

When I was close enough I bolted, easily taking down the animal I set my sights on. Before I could kill it, something collided with me, knocking me away from the animal and allowing it to run away, blood dripping from its neck wound.

I lost hold of my wolf form when I collided with the ground. The black wolf clamped its jaw down on my shoulder, keeping me in place as Erik became human. He kept his fangs. His claws dug into my wrists as he held me down.

'Erik.' I could hear the whine in my voice as I struggled to get free. I knew it was hopeless but I tried anyway cringing with pain.

***

I was shaking, hugging myself at the base of the tree he'd left me at. My wounds had healed but my entire body was sore. I don't know how long I laid there for. I had fought back the moisture in my eyes several times, it was better to stay angry with him, fear would only get me killed.

A howl ripping through the air broke me out of my stasis. 'Toby.' I forced myself to my feet and bolted in the direction of his howl.

When I broke out of the trees I was full wolf. It took only a few seconds to take in the scene before me. It appeared that Alec had decided to make an appearance during gym class. His government lackey in tow.

Toby was crouched on the ground, his skin rippling. All I could see was the electric rod in the man's hand. He moved it to strike again. Within seconds I was in between them. I had never experienced so much pain. Somehow I forced my hand to grab the rod as the pain increased. With a little effort, I pulled it from the man's grip.

Through it all I managed to keep my wolf form intact. I dropped the rod to the ground beneath me as I felt the electrical currents leave my body. I shook out my fur and lowered my head, ears flicking back, hackles raised. I growled, deeply and threateningly at the two humans in front of me.

They took a step back and I turned to face Toby. He'd lost it, he was shifting and he couldn't stop it. Moments later his russet wolf was in front of me, his torn clothes surrounding him on the ground.

The wolf dodged around me to attack the humans that hurt him. I leaped at him before he got there. My growl at Toby's wolf was less threatening, but it was more dominant as I stood over him. The wolf didn't move so I stepped back.

Toby rolled back onto his stomach and started to get up. The wolf had its sights on the two humans. Another dominant growl tore out of my throat and the wolf almost collapsed onto the ground, its ears flat and his tail close to Toby's canine body. The image of canine submission. This time when I moved, Toby didn't.

I turned so that I could keep the submissive wolf in sight. Instead of looking frightened, like most people would be in this situation, they looked curious. That just made me want to attack them. I held back another growl.

I would have preferred not to but I couldn't hold in my anger. I had to yell at them. I returned to human form, positioning my crouch on the ground so I hid the majority of my naked body from the watching humans. 'You two are a new kind of idiotic!' There was a definite rumble in my voice as I continued to fight the urge to snarl.

'What did you just do to him?' Alec asked, pointing

at the wolf. The wolf in question growled.

'Down,' I told the wolf, he resettled, obedient. I looked back at the idiots. 'If he hadn't have called me then you two would be dead now.'

'Your friend Toby doesn't look very dangerous.' The government man stated.

'Because I am one of the few people that can keep other werewolves under control,' I stated. 'He wouldn't dare stand up to me.'

'I was under the impression that schools were violence free zones.' Agua had come up beside me. 'Toby has never lost control before. You know about him for less than a day and here we are.'

'The trio,' Alec stated. 'You two went to great lengths to get her out of my lab.' He glanced at me. 'Even exposed yourselves.'

'I would do it again too,' Agua stated. 'The three of us have been together since we were kids. We're family.' She glanced at me. *'Where's your closest clothes?'* she asked silently.

'At home,' I responded, just as silent.

She took a deep breath and directed her hand at me. I had no idea what she was doing. That must have shown because she said. 'Just stay still.'

I did as she asked, staying as still as I could. After a moment, her hand glowed and I felt the magic swirl around me. Holy crap. One moment I was naked and the next I had clothes on, jeans, shirt, underwear and all. 'When did you learn that trick?' My surprise was clear in my voice.

'A while back. Haven't really had a chance to use it till now.'

'Cool.' I pushed myself to my feet. 'No, you get back down,' I growled at the wolf, it had started to stand. It collapsed with a soft whine, exposing his neck. 'If you didn't want this to happen you should have thought twice about letting yourself out.' I told the wolf. It looked up at me, instantly looking down again when our eyes met. 'You stay down until I tell you to get up.' Toby laid his head down on his paws.

I looked back at Hall. 'What will make you leave us alone?' I asked.

'Answers,' he said instantly.

'Fine,' I stated. 'But it ends with me. You leave everyone else alone.' I looked at the agent. 'No more shooting us with bullets, or electrocuting us. That shit hurts and can cause this.' I gestured at Toby, his ears flickered as he followed the movement.

'You seem fine,' Alec stated.

'Like I told you yesterday, I've been a werewolf a lot longer than Toby and Maya,' I reminded him. 'I have to be extremely angry or severely injured to even come close to losing control.' He didn't have to know about the whole Zac side of it.

'Let's go then.'

'No,' I stated. 'I have conditions to telling you anything about me.'

'What are those?' Alec seemed worried.

'I get to live my life,' I said flatly. 'Return to school, my home.'

'You want to go back to school?' There was disbelief in his voice. Right, what teenager wanted to go to school?

'It's my job,' I stated. 'I go to school to watch over

less experienced werewolves so nobody gets hurt. They go to socialise and learn control in real human situations.' He looked surprised by this. 'I can tell you that I know more about biology then you'll ever learn in your life time. I also have a vast knowledge in mechanical science and technological design.'

'You're sixteen.' There was complete disbelief in his voice now.

'No,' I said flatly. 'I'm eleven,' I looked down at the wolf. 'Toby studies computer science and molecular chemistry. We would get insanely bored if we stuck to the school curriculum.'

'What?' Alec said with disbelief.

I looked down at the wolf. 'Let's go.' The wolf got obediently to his feet.

'Where are you going?' he demanded.

'To take this wolf to eat so I can get Toby back,' I said flatly. The wolf walked silently a few steps to stand in front of me. He stopped when I did. I turned back to face Alec. 'I'm going to warn you now,' I stated. 'I know you took some of my blood when I was unconscious. Don't even think of putting it in a human body.'

'Why?'

I ignored his query. 'If you do, I will destroy every fragment of research you possess in that lab of yours.'

'Why?' he repeated.

I looked him in the eyes. 'I don't want to have to kill the human you infect.' I glanced at the patiently waiting wolf. Toby's wolf was reasonably mellow outside the dark moon. 'Do we have a deal?' I asked. 'I will answer your questions. Within reason. In return, you leave my pack alone.'

'Deal,' he said. I was kind of glad there were human witnesses to this little arrangement; it would force him to keep his word.

'Great,' I said. 'Now I'm going to go deal with this. I will come to you.' *Once I filled in the others*, I thought to myself.

'Do you want me to come with you?' Agua asked, looking at the wolf.

'I've got him,' I said. 'Meet me at the bunker. Your spell gave me an idea.'

Despite the situation, she smirked. 'Figures. Prepare yourself, nobody is going to see this one for days.' This last part she said louder.

I rolled my eyes. 'I'm not that bad.' She gave me look. 'Whatever... first I need to get Toby back. I need his computer science.' The wolf's ears flickered at the sound of his name. 'Go,' I said to the wolf. 'Run.' It hesitated before moving. It ran towards the forest. I followed. I hadn't realised how far away from the trees we had been. We were actually right near the school buildings.

Somehow Agua knew exactly when I was about to transform. I felt the magic ripple around me as I dove into wolf form. I snapped at Toby's ankles, making him move faster. The wolf obliged and we raced into the trees.

AGUA FRAY

I saw Hall's eyes set on me when Rya's clothes

appeared in my arms. I rolled them into a ball and turned away. I was expecting him to come running after me; I wasn't expecting him to touch me. He actually had the guts to touch me.

I spun around, using my leg to trip him. He fell flat on his back. I lifted my hand threateningly as small ball of purple light appeared in my palm. 'Just because I'm not a werewolf doesn't mean you can touch me,' I stated. 'And I might not be a werewolf but I'm still part of the pack. Which means, according to the deal you just made, I'm off limits.'

'What are you?'

'Something you don't want to cross.' I said. 'I will do a hell of a lot more then destroy your research.' I clenched my hand and let it fall to my side. 'Touch me again and I'll leave a mark.'

'What is Rya's idea?' he asked me.

'I can't know for sure,' I responded. 'No one ever knows until it's done or she needs them.'

'How is she only eleven years old?'

'She will answer your questions.' I saw little Hall walking up to us. 'You want to come?' I asked when he reached us.

'You want me to come?'

'Don't get me wrong, Rya will completely ignore you when she gets back, but I can fill in a few blanks for you.' He looked rather surprised. 'You helped us find Rya. It's the least we can do.'

'You helped her escape?' His father looked betrayed.

'I trust her,' Zac said.

'She's a werewolf.'

'I don't care,' Zac retorted. 'When I asked her why I shouldn't tell you she told me what you would do.' He shook his head. 'And you did exactly that. I don't even know what to think of you anymore.'

'Watch your tone with me,' Hall almost growled. 'I'm your father.'

'Right now, I don't care.' He looked at me. 'Let's go.' I could sense his anger.

Any other person would leave him here to sort it out with his father. Not me. This was one fight I wasn't going to stop. I put my hand on his shoulder. 'Hold your breath.' I let my magic envelop us as I envisioned the bunker. I clenched my free hand and we were sucked through the portal I created.

I stopped the human from falling when we landed. 'Oh shit, that was weird,' Zac said. He looked kind of nauseous.

'It'll pass.'

I walked over to the hatch in the ground. At this moment, it was covered. I moved the foliage away from the edges and pulled it open, waiting for Zac to go down first. When he reached the bottom and moved out of the way, I climbed down and pulled the hatch closed behind me.

RYA GARCIA

The table in front of us was strewn with paper: notes. Toby's laptop was between us. 'Agua can create a pocket for this to work,' Toby said, in a hushed voice. 'I can rig the software but we'll have to pinpoint the activation sequence according to transformation.'

'We can't overload the tech,' I reminded him. 'It will be small so it will be limited.'

He looked deep in thought. He grabbed a blank sheet of paper. 'Obviously it needs to have some kind of elasticity to it, otherwise it will come off as soon as we transform. What if it's linked?' He drew several rectangles about the size of my fingertip. They were in a straight line.

I saw where he was going with this. I reached over with my pencil. 'Each link can be an individual system to help support the software,' I agreed. I drew lines linking the rectangles together. 'I'm sure I'll be able to get my hands on a material that can act as a link between them and make a better connection without disrupting its elasticity.'

'The hard part is going to be sequencing it to the werewolf's transformation since everyone transforms at different rates.' Toby said.

'What if it has biometric sensors on the inside of the links?' I asked him. 'I can program them to read the body so it will activate at the right moment.' I wrote it down as I said it. 'The speed may be different but the body reacts in the same way, we just need to pinpoint the correct moment in both transformations.' My eyes scanned our notes. 'In theory this design should work, but it will take time to get the materials to make a prototype, I don't have all of these materials at the lab.'

'It will give me a chance to write the program.'

'I'll call in some of the others to help pinpoint the perfect time for it to activate.'

'Rya, Toby.' I was actually slightly startled by the voice in front of me. Judging by the way Toby suddenly looked up, he had also forgotten where we were.

'Miss Elms,' I responded, we weren't in the lab anymore. Toby's mother had come out of her office and told us to go to school.

'If you're finished keep it down,' she said.

'Sorry Miss,' we said together.

For the rest of the lesson we brainstormed silently. Talking to each other with our minds rather than our mouths. I had pulled out my laptop and started using a program we created for technology design. It would allow me to create a visual prototype while we waited for the materials. Toby had been scrawling all kinds of codes on the paper as he worked out the best way to create the program we would need.

When the bell rang we weren't expecting it. We both flinched, dragged out of our thoughts by the loud ringing in our ears. While the rest of our classmates gave their booklets to Miss Elms, Toby and I were sorting through the papers and dividing them up between us, depending on who needed them.

I left only a single sheet of paper out as I pulled my phone out of my pocket and chose a number out of the contacts list. It answered within minutes. 'Rya, how are you?' the husky male voice said on the other end. 'I heard what happened out there.'

'Hey, Harry,' I responded. 'It's a bit of a bummer but so far we're doing okay. How's the rest of the country taking our surprise revelation?'

'They're waiting to see if anyone else will slip up

and expose themselves.'

'I probably would have heard about if someone did.'

'Yeah, for now it's just you lot,' he admitted. 'So I know you didn't just call your old cousin for a chat.'

'You know me too well.' I gave Miss Elms the completed maths book. 'I need some materials.'

'What do you need?' I gave him my list. 'Standard stuff. I should have it all hanging around. When do you want it?'

'Sooner rather than later,' I told him.

'I'll see what I can get together and I'll send it out.'

'Thanks, cuz.'

'Be careful out there,' he told me, his tone a little more serious. 'The world just got a lot more dangerous for us.'

'I will. Bye.' I hung up. I pocketed the phone then grabbed my bag and my books. Not surprisingly, a few of our classmates had hung around to listen. This had been happening all day. Toby and I left the classroom, our lockers were just across from the maths room.

We stashed our books and our laptops inside and went to lunch continuing to talk about the device as we lined up for food in the cafeteria. I could sense the humans trying to listen but they wouldn't really understand what we were saying.

I grabbed a serving of chicken nuggets and chips, followed by a tub of gravy and a bottle of water. I paid and walked to the table where Agua sat with the others. I wasn't expecting to find Zac, Dylan and Sean sitting there too.

'I see you've ditched the cover-up,' Agua commented, her eyes looking over the jeans and tight tank top I wore.

'Why not?' I stated. 'I don't have to hide my strength anymore. Why shouldn't I ditch the baggy clothes? I hated them anyway.' I sat down beside her. I didn't want to overstep by sitting in the seat next to Zac. There was a moment of awkward silence when Toby took the remaining seat. Mostly the tension between the two of them.

'So I heard you two were inventing something,' Dylan said.

'Not really,' I told him.

'Not really,' Max said. 'You two have gone full nerd on us.'

'So you all knew?' Sean questioned the three freshmen at our table.

'Kind of,' Brian commented. I could sense his hidden amusement. I kind of felt amused by this myself.

'You're all werewolves.' Dylan at least had the sense to keep his voice down.

'You catch on quick,' Agua commented with a smirk.

'You're all werewolves.' Funny how Sean had so much disbelief in his voice.

'Well,' I said. 'Not yet.'

'What does that mean?' Sean asked.

I glanced at the others, they all shrugged. I looked back at the boys. 'Most of us turn in freshman year or early sophomore. Toby was a late sophomore year, Mira turned recently, while Max, Liam and Brian still have to turn.'

'What about you?' Dylan asked, looking at me.

'I turned six years ago,' I stated. I shook my head. 'It's a long story,' I said before he could ask. 'One I really don't feel like sharing.' He closed his mouth.

'So, is it true that you're only eleven?' Sean asked.

Why did I feel like rolling my eyes? 'Yes.'

'Feel like a paedophile yet?' Dylan had leaned forward to look at Zac.

Every supernatural at the table stopped themselves from laughing outright; except Toby, he kept a straight face. 'What?' Dylan looked both glad and confused by our reaction.

'It's nothing,' I told him. 'We joked about the same thing when Zac and I first started going out.' Instant awkwardness. I hated this. It was almost a relief when the bell finally rang. I gathered my now empty tray and was gone before the others really moved.

I didn't go far, I was waiting for Zac at his locker when he caught up. His two friends hesitated. 'Can we talk please?' I felt like I was begging. 'Privately.'

'When?'

Not a no. 'Now.' I knew he had a free period.

'Don't you have biology?' he questioned.

'Class can wait. This can't.' I was trying my best to ignore the watchful high school students.

It didn't take any more prompting. He followed me outside and into the forest out of sight. He only slightly hesitated when we crossed the tree line. I hoped it was because the last time he followed me in Erik attacked him.

I didn't go too far, just far enough that we were out of sight from the school. Even though the forest was my home field, I kept looking around, as if Erik was coming for me. I hadn't seen him since yesterday morning.

I leaned against a tree. Zac stayed facing me, and I could sense how anxious he was. There were several minutes of silence, neither of us seemed to know how to start. 'I'm sorry,' I finally said, beating down my pride. 'I'm sorry I didn't tell you who I was.'

'Judging by how I reacted, and what my father did, I don't really blame you for not trusting me,' he responded.

'My decision never had anything to do with not trusting you.' I told him. 'It was about protecting you from my world, especially Erik. I wanted to tell you, but it wasn't safe with him around.'

'So you weren't with me to get at my father?'

'No,' I answered truthfully. 'I would never do something that cruel.' A few silent moments later. 'Where does this leave us?'

'I don't know.' He crossed his arms. Not aggressively, more like he was hugging himself.

'I think we should start over,' I suddenly. I hesitated when he looked up at me. 'Except this time, you'll know.' I realised I was postured the exact same way, vulnerable.

I didn't expect him to come at me. His lips connecting with mine, a single hand under my chin while the other touched the tree behind me. Naturally I responded, my own hand went to his side at the base of his ribs.

When he released me, he spoke. 'I can't get Dylan's comment out of my head.'

I couldn't help it, I laughed. 'I'm sure you'll get over it.' I kissed him again. He didn't protest. We still had to sort out what we were, but at least we were a we. 'I have to go to biology,' I said when I broke away.

'Skip it,' he muttered into my cheek.

I hated to, I didn't want to. 'I like biology.' Reluctantly he released me. 'I'll see you later.' He nodded. 'Don't stay out here too long,' I warned. 'I

wouldn't put it past Erik to come after you again.'
When I walked out of the forest, he followed. Only
difference, he went to sit with Sean under our tree
while I went to the school building.

Our conversation went through my head as I
grabbed my books. We hadn't talked about his father,
we hadn't talked about much at all, we only knew that
we both wanted to work it out. For now, that was
good enough for me. The rest could come later.

A loud bark and growl broke me out of my
thoughts. I instantly turned to face it and took a step
back. I stopped myself from snarling at the canine.
There was a dog untethered, apparently it had been
sitting, now its ears were back, hackles raised as it
continued to growl at me. My heart was pumping
from the sudden change of pace.

'Nice of you to join us Rya,' Mr Harris said.

'Looks like someone isn't very trustworthy,' I
heard someone comment in the back of the room.

'That's actually a common misconception about
canine behaviour,' I told Jace, the culprit. I placed my
books on my empty table. 'She's not growling at me
because she doesn't like me. She's growling because
she's probably never come across someone like me
before.' I looked at Harris. 'One of your farm dogs I
presume.'

'How'd you know?' the teacher questioned.

'I've friended all the dogs in town,' I admitted. I
looked between Jace and my teacher. 'She's just
protecting herself, and her pups.' I looked deeply into
her eyes. Letting in just enough wolf to make my eyes
glow. Her tail dropped instantly, a whine escaping her

as she circled back to Mr Harris. She folded herself up next to the desk.

I took my seat, ignoring the following silence. I liked Mr Harris. He was kind to everybody. Other than being the Science teacher he was also the principal. He seemed to get that I wasn't looking to share with them so he continued his lesson on canine body language as if I hadn't just entered.

Once the class was silently going through textbook chapters he walked over to me. I had already finished it. 'You know part of coming to school means actually doing the work.'

I had my laptop open in front of me, watching an old transformation sequence from previous studies. It wasn't a real werewolf transforming. 'I read that book in two days at the start of term,' I told him, not taking my eyes off the screen.

'So you're really smart.'

'I will have to thank all you teachers for not revealing my grades to everyone,' I said. I wrote on one my pages of notes about the transformation sequence. The device should activate after the bones started shifting. 'I wasn't supposed to make my grades perfect, but I couldn't stand the thought of simplifying my answers or purposely getting them wrong.'

'How smart are you?' I couldn't smell anything but plain curiosity.

I put down my pencil and opened up four different transformation sequences. 'Werewolves have access to higher brain functions,' I said absently. 'It makes us abnormally smarter than humans and provides us with access to higher powers.'

'Are you telling me that it's possible for humans to access the same abilities?'

'Theoretically, yes,' I answered. 'Humans have the same capacity as werewolves, other than changing into a physical wolf of course. That's magic plain and simple.'

'How does a human reach that power?'

'They can't,' I said flatly. 'Human kind hasn't evolved enough to handle the pressure on the mind. I'm not even sure if humans have evolved enough to accept the shadow world. Not much has changed since last time.'

'Last time?'

I looked him in the eyes. 'You don't really think this is the first time one of us has been seen or caught.' I opened the information on the blood work throughout the different test subjects. I wanted some fresh results, particularly based on the blood work in the wrist and ankle.

'So how did you end up this way?' my teacher asked. He had always liked talking to me outside of class. 'Did you choose it or did somebody attack you?'

'I've been attacked by many things in my lifetime, none of them turned me into a werewolf.' I knew I wasn't giving him a straight answer.

'So you chose to become a werewolf.' He hesitated sightly on the last word.

'Choice never has anything to do with it if you were born this way,' I admitted. 'Turning humans is a big risk and is rarely done. Only the alpha can approve humans being introduced to the pack.'

'Who is that?' he asked.

'The black wolf I'm always fighting.' My voice was flat. 'He's not supposed to have the position.'

'Why? Isn't it the strongest that gets the top rank?'

'It doesn't work like that. Not in a true pack,' I responded. 'There are twelve true werewolf packs throughout America, true meaning run by the original family of werewolves,' I responded. 'Ours is a true pack, but he is not a werewolf from the original bloodline.'

'Who is?'

The bell rang and I quickly packed up my things and walked out of the room without answering.

'Hey,' I said when Zac sat next to me in the gym.

'How'd biology go?' he asked.

I shrugged. 'I survived.'

'Is that a good thing?' Toby sat on my other side, Agua only a moment behind him.

'Always a good thing.'

All four of us were wearing our gym clothes. Everybody wore the same school shorts and singlets for exercise. All of the girls wore sports bras underneath. Pretty much the only difference between my school gym clothes and my exercise clothes was the singlet.

'So, how'd you go?' I asked my two supernatural friends.

Agua smirked. 'I get the curiosity of nobody knowing what I am.' They knew the Fray's weren't werewolves, but nobody had actually confirmed what they really were.

'You not gonna tell them?' I questioned.

She shook her head. 'Let'em work for it.'

I didn't get to respond, because our teachers had arrived. Four of them for the entire grade. 'Okay everybody!' Mr Leeson shouted across the gym. 'As you all know we're starting our classes for self-defence. A useful thing to know when you go to places like the city.'

'Or when your town is infested with werewolves.'

'Trust me Jace,' I said before I could stop myself. 'If you come face to face with a werewolf that wants to fight you, no amount of martial arts training will help you.'

I sensed Toby smirk beside me.

'I've been doing martial arts since I was a kid. I'm a black belt. As if you could defeat me.'

'Maybe we should subject you to the kind of training I do every day,' I told him.

There was silence following my comment. 'Anyway,' Leeson said uncomfortably, 'let's get back to it.'

That recaptured everybody's attention. He continued to talk about how learning self-defence could help them if they ever got into a bad situation. They ended up breaking us up into groups. I was almost amused when the teachers didn't bother sorting me and Toby.

'So what are we supposed to do?' Toby asked mockingly.

I glanced at him. A smirk on my face. 'Fight,' I suggested.

I stood up from my seat on the bleachers. I jumped over the four rows of seats in front of me, landing easily on my feet. Toby landed beside me a moment later. 'Show off,' I stated in response to his flip.

We followed our classmates to the outside oval. It looked like the class would be taking place on the grass. Toby and I squared off against each other. We had left some space between us and the human students.

I waited for Toby to move. When he did I was ready for it. I blocked his blow and used my leg to trip him up. He fell flat on his back with a thud. I was really hating this singlet. It wasn't letting me move like I wanted.

Toby rolled to his feet and we squared off again. 'How do you move so fast?' Toby demanded.

'I use my size to my advantage,' I told him. 'Being smaller than most opponents I can be a lot faster.'

'But you flip and jump out of the way and strike back.'

'That takes practice,' I told him. 'I'll show you. Come at me with a high blow.' He did as I asked; I ducked underneath his incoming arm. I flipped and landed on my feet coming up to strike him in the back with my hands. 'By using this technique, you can get behind your opponent and strike back before they can recover.'

'Come at me from a low point,' I said as he turned around to face me again. Before he started moving I took the singlet off and tossed it a few metres away, leaving myself clad only in shorts and the sports bra. Toby rolled his eyes and did the same.

When he came at me this time, a low attack as requested, I leaped over him in the same manner as before. I turned around and grabbed him from behind, my arm wrapped around his neck. 'This way is easier,' I admitted.

I let him go and he massaged his neck. I wasn't

much shorter, but still short enough that I pulled him down whenever I did that. 'If you can predict what type of attack your opponent will make then you can get behind them and strike them.

'Seems easy enough,' he speculated.

I shrugged. 'It takes practice. Have a go.'.

We squared off again. I was vaguely aware that a few of our classmates were watching. I came forward first. I went for the high blow. I hated obvious attacks, they were pointless. Toby moved forward a moment later diving beneath my attacking arm.

He lost it on the tight flip, hitting the ground rather than landing on his feet. 'It's harder than it looks,' Toby stated.

'Yeah it is,' I admitted, staring down at him. 'You have to stay low, but not too low, otherwise you end up on the ground and leave yourself open to attack.'

We reset ourselves. 'I'll go low,' I told him. 'So you jump.'

We did exactly that. I went low and he leaped over the top of me, I stood up and his hand wrapped around my throat. 'It is easier,' he stated.

I smirked. 'So what happens if a fight gets to this point?' I asked him.

'Nothing,' he answered, dropping his arm. 'It's over.'

'Not necessarily,' I responded. 'Wrap your arm around again and hold it as if in a real fight.' He did so. 'If you're in this position you can use their body weight to your advantage.'

To demonstrate I grabbed the arm that was around my throat. I dove forward again, flipping and landing on my feet. The only difference Toby was on the ground. I looked down at him with a smirk. 'Hurts, doesn't it?'

He took my hand and I helped him to his feet. 'What did you do?'

'When somebody comes up behind you like that they expect to have the advantage,' I explained. 'If you have enough strength of your own you can pull them into a flip with you, and in most cases, it will cause them to let go. Giving you the chance to get free and make another attack.'

He stepped forward. 'No, you're not going to try it with me,' I stated. 'I don't really want to hit the ground a dozen times while you practice.' Toby smirked at my comment. 'You need to practice your low flip.'

'How low?' he asked me.

'As low as you can get,' I said.

I turned and walked over to Agua as Toby started working on that one. 'How's your training been going?' I asked her casually.

'Done with him, now you're after me?' she grinned, despite her serious tone.

'Any new offensive spells?' Most of what she knew was defensive, she was only just getting into offense.

'A few,' she admitted. 'You wanna have a go?'

I shrugged. 'I could use a proper workout.' I glanced at the humans. They weren't close enough to hear our conversation but they were watching occasionally. 'And since we still have time left in class, you can get some practice.'

'You know not all of us are masters of the fighting

arts.' Her voice was full of mock anger.

I grinned. 'Do you want to or not?'

'Of course,' she responded.

I took several steps back. I then grabbed the tie out of my pocket and tied my hair into a tight bun, my hair would just get in the way. 'So what are we playing with today?' I called out.

I saw her mouth move, but I didn't hear the whispered word. I couldn't stop my surprise when a long tendril of fire erupted from her outstretched hand. It wrapped a wide circle around me. It was purple in colour, the colour of her magic.

'When did you learn to do that?' I asked, looking around me at the rippling flames.

They faded, only the slightest amount of heat remaining of their existence. 'We've been working on it for a while now,' Agua answered. 'It took me a few weeks to get the hang of it.'

'This could be fun,' I said it just loud enough to hear, she grinned again. 'But let's not set the place on fire.'

She threw a new tendril out towards me. Straight into it. I ducked and rolled beneath the flame. I felt the heat rush over me. This was crazy. It was weird not having something to hit. That's what made this good training, it made me use my instincts.

Agua soon added a second tendril of flame, wrapping them around me, making it more and more difficult to escape the fire. Then she had to make it more difficult. The next time I turned around a pillar of earth shot out of the ground in front of me.

It wasn't large, but I did have to stop myself from

turning into it. 'Throwing obstacles in now, are we?' Agua just smirked, she only looked slightly worn.

We continued on, except now I had to watch out for her strong pillar made out of... I wasn't really sure what it was made out of. Soon another one appeared. I barely had time to register that it was there, protruding out of the ground maybe two metres from the other.

I leaped at one to dodge the flames, the heat and exertion making my body sweat. I clung onto the pole, but I had to leap to the other one to dodge another strip of fire. Even then I had to kind of swing myself around it to dodge Agua's attack.

The pace was definitely starting to wear on me. Before she could attack me, I went back to the other post. I grabbed the top of the earth like pole and used it the propel myself towards Agua. I had to drop to the ground as she moved her flames in my direction.

I skidded across the ground doing my best to ignore the searing pain across my arm as I leaped at her. She lost her grip on her magic when she hit the ground. The flames disappeared and I heard the earth pillars crumble and fall back to the ground.

I didn't hold her down like I did with Toby. I rolled onto my back and laid down beside her, breathing heavily from the exertion. I didn't have to glance at her to know she was the same way. I lifted my right arm so I could inspect it. 'You burnt me,' I said, a tone of accusation in my voice.

'Poor baby,' she said in a mock soothing voice. 'Do you want me to fix it for you?' She sat up. She was serious about the healing part.

I laughed, forcing myself into a sitting position. 'Save your strength. It's not that bad.'

I didn't hear what she said in response because a sudden piercing feeling went through my mind. I stopped my growl of pain as it dug deeper, my hand pressing into my temple. It was like somebody had thrust a knife through my consciousness and was slowly cutting away pieces. 'Something's in my head.'

I felt Agua's hand on my shoulder, her voice only a mumble. I couldn't focus on that. I clenched my teeth as I wrapped my mind around the intruder. Once I was sure the intruder was caught, I thrust out with all the strength I could muster.

I stayed still for a moment, making sure that whatever it was, was gone. My mind felt raw. Whoever it was had been prying back the layers of my mind, searching for something. 'Rya?' Agua's voice broke through my own searching.

I shook my head clearing it. Then I looked over at her. 'It's gone,' I told her.

'I figured,' she stated. 'Did you have to throw me?' It took me a moment to realise that she was several feet away.

'Sorry,' I told her. 'Something was digging through my head. I had to force it out.' I pushed myself to my feet.

'You're going to find it, aren't you?' she questioned.

She knew me too well. 'Yes,' I said flatly. 'If there's an intruder in our territory then I need to find it.'

'Ry!' Toby called out. He nodded to the tree line when I glanced at him. He was backing away from it, refusing to turn his back.

A woman was leaning against a tree. It only took a moment to register that it wasn't human. 'You werewolves always leave your minds open when you think you're safe.' She looked familiar, but I couldn't figure out why.

'I didn't realise I had to close my mind in my own territory,' I shot back. 'Don't you know this town is off limits to your kind?'

'Funny,' she sneered. 'That didn't stop me from coming and going six years ago.'

Six years ago? It took me a moment. 'You were with him?' My words came out like a growl.

'Good job, pup,' she said. 'He sends his regards and told me to tell you that he will see you soon sweetheart.'

That last word sent chills down my spine. It was also the moment where I was done listening to her speak. I closed the distance between us in seconds. She didn't resist me as I slammed her against the tree she had been standing in front of. 'Where is he?' I growled.

'Not yet honey.' She smirked, probably glad that she had struck a nerve. 'He says you're not ready.'

I heard a shift in the branches above me. I should have known she wouldn't be alone. 'Why now?' I asked. 'If he wanted to kill me why would he wait six years to come back?' She didn't respond as I glanced into the trees above me. I counted six. 'So why are you here? You had to know that I would kill you.'

'If you're strong enough.'

'I've been hunting vampires since I became a

werewolf,' I growled. 'I am also one of the strongest werewolves in this town.'

My hand was still wrapped around her throat. 'You seem to talk more then you fight.'

'Because unlike your kind, killing isn't a habit we like to make. You're nothing but a bunch of parasites.'

She didn't like that comment. She hissed at me, her fangs appearing on her canines extended. I clenched my hand shut, ripping through the skin as I pulled. Every piece of her disintegrated making a cloud of ash that drifted to the ground at my feet.

As expected her companions dropped out of the trees, surrounding me. They all came at me at once. I ducked and slid through a gap between two of them. Before I had a chance to stop I turned around and grabbed one.

I wrapped my arm around its throat and pulled. There was a resounding crack just before it disintegrated. I ducked again and shoved the opposing female into a few of her companions, giving me the chance to kill another.

I killed two more in the same manner. I pinned the next one at the same moment the remaining vampire attached itself onto my back. Those long sharp fangs pierced my neck at the same moment I killed her friend.

I stood up, despite the extra weight on my back. I did what I had shown Toby earlier, a tight somersault in the air. Except the vampire didn't let go. It just continued to drain the blood out of my neck. The sudden blood loss was luring my wolf towards the danger.

I shook my head to clear it before doing another somersault. This time we hit the ground. Its arm moved from around my neck and I lashed out, my teeth closing around the limb. Only good thing about vampires, they didn't bleed, but they tasted disgusting, like rotting flesh.

The parasite let go, shouting out in pain as I rolled away without her added weight. Within seconds I was at her throat, my own fangs bared and a growl rumbling in my chest. 'Tell me what I want to know and I'll kill you quickly.' I spoke around my elongated canines, ignoring the wolf that pushed at my layers of control.

'I can't tell you anything.' She growled.

I glanced at the bite on her arm, her flesh was already turning a grey colour. 'You're dying anyway,' I informed her.

'I don't know anything,' she whined. 'That woman you killed first, Angela. She turned me a few weeks ago, told me that I had to help her. Please… let me go.' The girls voice was a whine now.

'I can't do that,' I told her. 'You feed off the living, and you've tasted my blood. It's the only thing you'll crave now. Human blood won't satiate your thirst, and you'll come after me and my family.'

The greying of her skin had spread rapidly, it was now reaching her chest, having covered her arm. When it did finally reach that pivotal part of her body, she screamed in pain. 'I'm sorry she did this to you, but I have to protect my own.' I took her life with the clenching of my claws into her throat.

I didn't stand up. I didn't think I had enough

energy to do that. After all the training, the fight and the blood loss, my energy was gone. Vampires were turning humans not much older than my classmates.

I slipped into a more comfortable sitting position and leaned my elbow on my elevated knee. I flinched when a hand touched my shoulder. I mean, not just a little flinch, like an overreaction. One moment I was sitting on the ground and the next I had grabbed the person and dumped them on the ground beneath me.

I stopped, my hand raised, claws out, ready to attack. I let Zac go, getting to my feet. He was staring up at me, more shock on his face then anything. I could also sense the slightest hint of worry, but also fear. I turned towards the forest at the same moment the school bell rang.

I walked past Toby, he had crept closer since the fight. I think he expected me to hand him my phone and wallet because he took them the moment I handed them over. The moment I was over the tree line I dove into my wolf form and broke into a run.

AGUA FRAY

It was unlike Rya to transform before disappearing from sight. That just showed how much wolf she used in that fight. The humans knew it too. Toby turned around to face Zac. 'You stupid, idiotic human,' He growled.

'I was making sure she was okay,' Zac responded.

'She was fine,' the werewolf returned. 'But for a fight like that, Rya would have had to access her wolf without transforming.'

Zac got to his feet, refusing to back down. I had to admit that he had guts for a human, standing up to a werewolf. 'Toby don't start.' I stepped in between them.

'I don't know why we tell him anything if he's still going to do stupid shit like this,' Toby glared at him over my head.

'Just leave him alone. Rya trusts him, so I do too.'

I turned slightly as Toby stalked past me. 'Just be glad that Rya has better control then the rest of us,' he growled as he passed the human. He continued across the oval and disappeared back into the gym.

'Where is she going?' Zac asked me.

'Honestly, I don't know for sure,' I admitted. 'The training and the fight would have taken a lot out of her.' He waited. I sighed, what a pushy kid. 'She's probably gone to eat, then she'll go home and sleep.'

Zac's friend Dylan had crept closer. The rest of our human classmates had started heading towards the school, they were ready to leave for the day. 'Next time,' I said in the silence, walking forward, 'don't sneak up on a werewolf.' I paused. 'That's how you get killed.'

ZAC HALL

I was sitting on her mailbox, waiting. I didn't even know if she was going to come back here. For all I knew she would sleep in the forest. I just needed to check on her. Somehow I'd managed to convince Dylan to go do something else. He had been sticking to me like a bur. He still hadn't fully forgiven me for not telling him about Rya.

'Hey.'

I started when her voice broke my thoughts. She looked exhausted. 'Hey.' She surprised me by taking my hand and pulling me off the mailbox. I thought I saw a smile on her lips before she turned away. I followed her into the house, led mostly by her soft grip on my hand.

'Have you eaten?' she asked letting go so she could sit on the couch.

I nodded, sitting down beside her; I'd stopped at home before coming over. 'Have you?' I asked.

'Yes.' was the response I got.

'So what happened out there today?' I questioned. I sort of knew, but I wanted to know more.

She took a deep breath. 'Sorry, I pinned you.' She was avoiding the question.

'Are you going to tell me what she said to you?' I asked, my voice soft. We hadn't been able to hear what the vampire and Rya had been saying before the fight.

Her eyes snapped up to mine. 'You're better off not knowing.'

She was leaning lazily against the cushion. She honestly looked like she was going to fall asleep.

'So what should we do?' I asked her.

She blinked, like she had been deep in thought. After a moment, she shrugged. 'We can watch a movie,' she answered. 'There're some in that case over there.'

I was fine with anything, I just wanted to get back to where we were before I found out. Since finding out about the whole werewolf side, things had been a little tense. I went over to the case, flicking through the dozens of dvds.

I smirked, and held up a disc to show Rya. She was watching me. She just rolled her eyes at the cover. 'The Howling?' she questioned. 'You pick a werewolf movie?'

'Hey, you're the werewolf watching werewolves,' I joked.

'I've never actually seen it,' she responded.

I got to my feet. 'All the more reason to watch it.'

'Fine.' She got to her feet and led the way to her room. It was easier to watch the wall mounted tv that mostly hid in the corner of her room. That and I think she just wanted to lay down. Sure enough, she pretty much collapsed onto the bed.

I had never seen her this tired before. It was actually kind of... 'Glad you're enjoying my exhaustion,' she stated, rolling over so she was on her back.

'How... never mind.' I think I was getting used to this reading the emotions thing. I put the movie in and jumped onto the bed beside Rya. She stayed quiet as I sifted through all the menus to get to the movie. I knew why. I had glanced at her after putting the remote on the bedside. She was fast asleep, flat on her back. I stopped myself from laughing and laid back to watch the movie.

RYA GARCIA

I woke, sitting upright on the bed. I rubbed my temples, my arm sitting on my raised knee. It felt like I had a hangover, my head was pounding. I started when something moved beside me. I forced myself to relax. Zac looked at the bedside. 'I don't mean to say anything but we were meant to be at school ten minutes ago.'

Shit. I went straight into the closet and grabbed out some clothes. 'Here,' I threw him a set.

'Aren't these Toby's?'

'Do you want to go to school in yesterday's clothes? Unless you brought some with you.' The look on his face told me he hadn't planned to stay the night. 'There's a shower in the other room.' I closed the bathroom door behind me. A few minutes later I heard the other shower start up.

After a hot shower and a quick breakfast, I was feeling almost human again. I still had a headache but at least it was slowly going away. He started in the direction of the school. I caught his hand. 'This way's faster.' He didn't let go of my hand as we walked into the forest.

We walked in silence. I could sense his hesitation, and it confused me. What was he wanting to do or say? He was getting used to entering he forest, even with Erik still skulking around, so it wasn't that. I left it.

Just before the school came into view, Zac stopped us. I turned to face him. 'What's wrong?'

He surprised me by pulling me closer, his hand reaching up to cradle my face. I almost expected it when he leaned in to kiss me. I turned my head slightly. 'Are you sure this is what you want?' I asked, my mouth near his ear.

'Yes.' He turned my head so I was looking up at him. 'I want to go back to how things were. But no more secrets.'

'I can't promise that.' My voice was soft. My wolf was urging me forward; this was what we wanted.

'Please?' he said. 'I want to know everything.'

'We should be going. We're late.' What was I doing?

He didn't let me move. I gave up. The wolf won. Zac seemed to realise this because he took his chance. He pressed his lips to mine, softly at first, then more deeply, and my body responded, almost of its own volition.

I heard the bell ring and I pulled away, taking a breath. 'We should go,' I told Zac against my wolf's wishes.

'I have a free period,' he responded pulling me back. I couldn't stop myself from responding as he kissed me again.

I shocked myself when I pushed him back against the tree behind him. Every part of me was urging me forward. I placed my hand on the tree to support myself, the other hand closing around the back of his neck.

I could feel his smile as his lips touched my neck, tenderly running a tingling trail. He ran his hand up my body. By this time, I was biting my lip, not enough to break the skin but enough to keep me grounded.

The bark cracked under my hand. I pulled away, not a lot, just enough to stop him. I knew that my eyes were glowing, I could see the reflection in Zac's own eyes. He would have heard the crack. I took a deep breath as the claws quickly shrank back to ordinary human nails.

'Rya,' I heard Colby's voice behind me. I turned away from Zac to face the lone werewolf. Only Colby wouldn't comment on what had just happened. 'We have a problem,' he said.

I glanced at Zac. 'Guess I'm not going to school yet.'

He smiled and pulled himself off the tree. 'I'll see you later then.' He kissed me again, briefly but softly. I saw him glance at Colby before heading in the direction of the school.

'That's going well I see.'

'Shut up,' I said to the smirking werewolf. He continued to grin as he turned around. I couldn't help my own contentment as I followed Colby back into the forest.

ZAC HALL

'Where have you been?' Dylan asked when he found me at my locker.

'Around.' I didn't need to tell him.

I gasped as I was shoved up against the lockers. 'Where's Rya?' Toby's voice echoed with a growl.

'Why are you questioning me?' I returned.

'Nobody has seen her since she left here yesterday,' he growled. 'Agua told you where she would be.'

'Get off me.' I smacked him in the chest with my hands, shoving him backwards a few steps.

He rushed forward. I had seen him fight enough to deflect his blow. My fist that followed hit him in the jaw. He stumbled back, I think more shocked then anything. 'You're not the only one that knows how to throw a punch.'

'You just made a big mistake.' Toby wiped the blood from the corner of his lip.

Before he had even taken a step forward the air rippled between us, it spread and surrounded Toby. He banged his fist on it. He couldn't get through. 'Let me go Agua,' Toby growled.

'No.' The girl pushed through the crowd of humans. 'He hasn't done anything wrong.'

'How do you know?' he asked.

'Because I just got a call from Colby. Rya is with him.'

I gave Toby a smug look. I didn't need to be a werewolf to sense his anger. 'Why can I smell her on you then?' he questioned me.

'Because I was with Rya when Colby came and got her.'

'Why?'

'Why what?'

'Why did Colby come and get her?'

'I don't know,' I said. 'He didn't say anything.'

'What about Rya?'

'That's none of your business.' The bell rang. Class time already. I closed my locker door. 'Come on, let's go.' I said as I walked past Dylan.

'You proud of yourself?' I heard Agua say behind me. 'You just made yourself look like an idiot.' I couldn't help but smirk. I just punched a werewolf in the face.

RYA GARCIA

When we reached Colby's destination I had to cover my nose and mouth. I'd smelled a dead body before but nothing like this. In the middle of the forest clearing was a young girl, she looked maybe ten.

'Who is it?' I asked, grimacing as the smell broke through my senses.

He shrugged. 'I won't know until I can ID her.'

'Who have you told?'

'Just you?'

'Good.' It would give us a chance to scope out a scent, without human contamination.

We didn't have to tell each other what to do, we just did it. Walking back to outside of the clearing and slowly making our way around in a circle. 'So, you and Zac seem to be going better.' I heard his voice from across the clearing.

'He's trusting me again,' I admitted. 'I didn't think that would happen so soon.'

'I think he's trying to do more than trust you.' I could hear the slightest hint of amusement in his voice.

'That… was unexpected.'

We stayed silent as we walked around. 'I heard about the vamp attack yesterday.' Colby said after a few minutes of silence. We had passed each other once already. 'Sorry I wasn't there to help.'

'I handled it fine.'

'Agua told me that one of the vampires was there the night your parents died.'

'Yes. She was.' She hadn't been in the dream from last night, but I do remember her being there. Sometimes she was in the dream sometimes she wasn't.

'Are you okay?'

Usually this was the time I said that I was fine, but Colby always knew better. I didn't hide things from Colby. 'I've been dreaming about that night the last few days,' I admitted. 'Then she turns up and says that he's coming for me. Not yet, but soon.'

'Isn't this what you've been training for?' he asked me. 'You push yourself to the limits nearly every day so that you'll be strong enough.'

'But what if I'm not strong enough?' I asked. 'He took out both of my parents. My father was one of the strongest and my mother wasn't exactly weak.'

We stopped, we had reached each other. 'You'll be ready,' he responded. 'But first we've got to get out from under Erik. Let's focus on that fight first. Who knows, maybe that's what this creature is waiting for?'

'And if it is?'

'Then we handle it together.' He touched my cheek softly, I leaned into the comforting touch. 'As a pack.' He pulled me into his arms. 'We're not going to lose another alpha to this thing. I think it might just destroy us.' He kissed me on the forehead. 'Now let's get this done so we can get away from the smell.'

Without another word, we continued in our spiral. Whatever this thing was it was good. It had ripped into the intestines, making it almost impossible to smell anything else. 'Ry,' Colby called out. 'Over here.'

I gave the body a wide birth as I crossed the clearing to where Colby stood. He was looking down into the dirt: a paw print.

'Spread out,' I suggested.

This time we went outwards until we found the trail. Definitely werewolf. 'Do you want to get the others?' I asked Colby. 'I'll warn the sheriff.' He nodded, grabbing out his phone. By others I meant, Keith and the twins. They were our fastest and strongest, great for tracking.

I turned around and ran in the direction of the police station. Surprisingly it wasn't that far. Just a short run. When I entered everyone looked at me. I felt like I stank of carrion. It would take several showers for me to feel clean again.

'Can I help you?' the woman at the desk asked.

'Sheriff Connors please.'

'I'm afraid he's in a meeting at the moment.'

I raised an eyebrow. 'Then get him out of the meeting, because this is important.'

She pursed her lips, but she got up and walked down the hallway to the conference room. I knew it was the conference room because I had been in there once before. 'What do you want?' The Sheriff didn't seem happy, his day wasn't going to get any better.

I indicated out the door. 'Privately.'

I could sense both his interest and his worry as he followed me back out the doors. When I was sure nobody was listening I told him about the girl. He seemed shocked by it all. 'Why didn't Colby tell me this?'

'He's tracking the scent we found.'

'How long ago did you find it?'

'Colby found the body an hour ago.' I answered.

A flush of anger. 'He should have reported it instead of going to you.'

'You would have trampled every piece of evidence the moment your team got there. As it was the creature covered its tracks. We were lucky to find a scent to follow.'

'So this is you telling us to clean it up?'

'This is me keeping things in the open,' I responded. He raised an eyebrow. 'We aren't hiding supernatural deaths from you anymore.'

'So what are you wanting me to do?'

'I can take your team out to the body so they can do their jobs. Colby may have left already, but he might be waiting for the others.'

'Come on.' He led the way back inside. 'Okay, everyone.' His voice easily reaching every corner of the room. 'I need two officers, a forensics and the coroner.' He looked down at me. 'Where are they heading?

'About a mile south,' I told him.

'Got anything better than that?'

'It's the middle of the forest, what do you expect?' I turned away. 'Just make sure they're armed, we don't know where this thing is.' I walked back out the door, deciding to wait for them outside. It took them only a few minutes to come out.

The coroner had a stretcher in his hands, the forensics guys were holding two bags while the… four officers, had rifles over their shoulders. 'I thought you were sending two,' I said when Connors appeared.

'If something's still out there then I want them to be protected.'

'This is a werewolf,' I stated. 'I can guarantee that those guns will just make it mad.' I looked over his shoulder into the precinct. 'Where's Colby's desk?'

'Back left corner… Why?'

I didn't answer I just re-entered the office and walked over to the desk. I sniffed, knowing that I would find them here somewhere. I followed my nose to the tang of silver. He used the silver ones so that it would look different to ordinary copper bullets.

Sorry Colby. I thought as I snapped open the cupboard door. I pulled out six clips. 'Here.' I said to the officers when I returned outside. 'Put these in your glocks. They will make a better weapon against this thing if it decides to show up.' I tossed one to each of them. 'Shoot me and I'll kill you.'

After a moment they grinned. 'I'm not joking,' I stated. They turned serious. 'Hit me with one of those and it will kill me, but before it does my wolf will rip her way out and take everyone else down with her.'

An officer opened his mouth to speak. 'No, it's not silver,' I stated before he could ask. 'Actually, the bullets are silver but it's not the silver that will kill me. Those bullets are made special and can kill most supernaturals. For an instant kill aim for the head or the heart.' It seemed like they understood. Without another word, I led them into the forest.

I set a fast pace putting us at the scene ten minutes later. I gave the spare clips to the officers as Colby came up to me. Apparently they hadn't left yet. 'Please stay away from that area over there,' he told his colleagues. He pointed to where we found the scent.

'Why?' one of the officers asked.

'That's where the scent is,' I told them. 'We're waiting for back up before we start tracking it.'

'Keith is caught up at work and can't get away, but the twins are on their way,' Colby told me in a hushed voice.

I looked at him. 'Do they know there are humans here?'

'I warned them. They'll transform so they don't see them as humans.'

I nodded. 'Are you going to be okay with the three of you?'

'I would prefer four of us, but nobody else is free. I checked.'

'What about me?' I questioned.

'We need someone to stay here with them.' He

nodded to the men. 'They're deep enough into the forest that Erik might come sniffing.'

'And we don't need a bunch of dead cops to deal with,' I agreed.

We heard the trotting of paws through the underbrush. We weren't the only ones. 'Weapons down,' Colby ordered as the two sandy wolves came into view. Charlie and Charlotte.

'Are you staying human?' I asked Colby, aware that the humans were focused on us now that the two sandy wolves had shown up.

'Not this time,' he answered. 'This thing has several hours head start. We need speed if we're going to catch up.'

To prove his point, he pulled his shirt easily over his head. He pulled a gun out of the back of his jeans and handed it to me. I despised the things. Maybe because I'd been shot one too many times. Colby turned away from his colleagues as his skin started to ripple with bluish black fur. He undid his jeans and his changing body easily slipped out of them without ripping the fabric.

'Sure you don't want me out there with you?' The wolf gave me a look. I could hope. I was stuck babysitting the humans. He didn't say anything he just led the other two towards the scent we had found.

I shook my head and picked up Colby's clothes, I half folded them tucking the gun inside and tossed them to the base of a nearby tree. 'Go on,' I told the officers. 'The quicker you guys finish up the quicker you can get back to town.'

The four officers spread out around the clearing perimeter. 'That's really cool,' the officer closest to me commented. I looked at him. 'You guys being werewolves I mean.'

I recognised him, more his scent then his face. 'You're Nate' I stated. 'Colby's partner.'

'How'd you know?' Nate asked.

'He's mentioned you a few times.'

He seemed surprised and happy about this information. 'So you enjoy being a werewolf?' he questioned.

'As much as anyone can,' I responded. 'There're a few downsides, but we can't just change what we are. So we make do.'

'You and Colby are close, aren't you?'

'He took care of me,' I responded. 'He's helped me through a lot.' Colby always kept me grounded. I could trust him to help me, no questions asked, most of the time.

It took them about an hour to cordon off the clearing. There was no sign of anything coming our way. Colby appeared just as we were packing up to leave, their fur was wet. When they stopped they shook the water out of their fur.

I grimaced as the spray hit me. Colby walked over to where I had put his clothes. I stood in front of him, the two sandy wolves doing the same, shielding his naked body as he returned to human form. He didn't speak until he stood up. 'You guys can head to the border,' he told the twins. 'I'll come relieve you at dusk.'

They ran off into the trees. Colby didn't put his

shirt back on, instead he used it to dry his hair. 'Did you find anything?' I asked him.

'It crossed the river a few miles out,' he stated. 'It must have travelled through the water to hide its scent.' He seemed disappointed. 'We followed the river and did a perimeter sweep, that wolf is either hiding in the deep woods or its gone.'

'You went around the lake.'

'Yes,' he said. 'We couldn't find an exit point. I didn't want to go into the deep woods without a full team.'

'It's fine,' I told him. 'If it comes back we'll know.'

'For now, I think we should set up patrols,' Colby recommended. 'I talked to those two on the way back.' Meaning the twins. 'It won't take much to get Keith and Lexi on board.' The last part was in a lowered voice so the humans didn't hear names.

I nodded. 'You realise this means I'm not going to get much sleep until we find this thing.'

'You and me both.'

We stood silently for a moment. 'Come on,' I said. 'These guys are pretty much ready to go.'

Nobody talked as we walked back to the precinct. When we got back I wasn't expecting to see a crowd of people. Apparently word of the child's death had spread. The two local news stations were there, so was a crowd of worried adults.

Connors was at their head. He seemed overwhelmed by the crowd. The officers ignored them. Colby and I however, hesitated. Colby was still shirtless, having made his shirt wet. And me, well everyone knew about me.

The Sheriff saw us before everyone else did, but his gaze caused the crowd to turn around. I wasn't really expecting the reporters to rush forward. I had to stop my wolf from snarling; they weren't attacking me, not really anyway.

Colby closed his hand around mine and pushed through the crowd, ignoring the humans that didn't seem to care that we were werewolves. So many questions were being thrown into my head. What happened to the girl? What was our involvement? Was she killed by something inhuman?

By the time we reached the doors my wolf was on the surface. Judging by the smell of Colby, he was feeling about the same. At least inside the precinct nobody was crowding us. We both took deep breaths, calming the wolves that had risen to the surface.

'Hey,' Colby said before the rest of the team could walk off. He held his hand out. 'Bullets?'

They each returned their unused super bullets. Colby already had the two spares in his shirt. I followed him to his desk and he stashed the bullets back into the broken cabinet. Then he pulled a fresh shirt out of a bag in the corner. One of the black shirts he wore under his uniform. He didn't even comment on the broken door.

'So what's next?' I asked him, leaning against the edge of his desk.

He was writing notes down about the case. For his report I guessed. 'I suggest you get some rest,' he said. 'You and I'll take over for the twins at dusk.'

'If the next shift starts before dawn it will allow me to get some more sleep before school,' I told him.

'Yeah that was my thinking,' he said. 'We really need more wolves to work with.'

'Unfortunately we're all that's left. I know that Toby wants in so I've been teaching him a few extra things, but he's not ready to go out on his own.'

'Should we bring in a few extras?'

I shrugged. 'They chose other jobs for a reason,' I told him. 'We keep our three shifts and put everyone else on alert. If it's still in the territory we'll know soon enough.'

'I don't think it would be a good idea to put the others on patrol. They only fight when necessary. I want to keep it that way.'

'Same,' I admitted. 'If we can work out a shift that we can all work to then it would be great.'

'I'll work something out,' he said. 'But for now we've got to deal with outside then rest up for tonight's shift.'

I glanced at the crowd. 'I think I'd rather face the rogue.'

'Same. I was kind of hoping we would find it.'

I turned my gaze back to his. 'Colby Martin are you itching for a fight?' I joked, he grinned.

He didn't respond, maybe because his colleagues were listening. He was one of the werewolves that needed to exert energy, otherwise he got tense and lost it. It'd happened a few times in the past. It's one of the reasons he took up law enforcement.

Connors came through the door and walked up to us. 'Are you two going to explain what happened?'

'Not if they're going to throw themselves at us,' Colby stated.

'I'll let them know to do this civilly.' The man turned around and went back outside. The Sherriff seemed to be taking his deputy's sudden werewolf status very easily.

After a few moments we followed Connors outside. They were waiting for us. I thought they were going to rush us again, and was glad they didn't. Colby stepped front and centre and I stood beside him.

'Okay everybody,' he said in a loud voice. 'Listen up carefully because I'm only explaining it once.'

'Yes, there has been a death. Yes, it was caused by the supernatural.' He seemed to avoid saying it was a werewolf.

'What is her involvement?' somebody asked suddenly.

'Rya and I lead a taskforce that works during these cases. We track the creature and assess the situation before making a decision.' And before anybody could ask. 'Yes, like Rya I am a werewolf.' There was a mixture of reactions, surprise, fear, curiosity.

'You were shirtless before... Why?' I guess we'd gotten to the questions part of this little thing.

'My shirt was wet.' I could have laughed at the answer if the situation wasn't so serious. 'We tracked it to the river a few miles out before it decided to cover its scent. We were unable to find an exit point.'

'So it's still out there?'

'We can hope that it was an isolated incident when it was passing through.' Colby was in full cop mode now. 'We're putting round the clock patrols and all of our people are on alert. If it's still here, we'll find it.'

'How did you find it?'

'I was heading out for a run.' Colby admitted. 'I caught the smell and went to investigate.'

'Why aren't you in uniform?' They were picking now.

'I'm not on duty,' he paused. 'And in cases like these, I prefer not to be.'

'So what do you do in a case like this?' Finally a decent question.

'We hunt, we find, we assess,' Colby answered. 'If it is hostile towards us we will put it down. If it is a danger to people, we will put it down. But first we try and rehabilitate and give it some kind of control.'

'It's killed a kid.'

'It could have been an accident. The attack was pretty brutal,' I stated as I stepped forward. 'If the werewolf is new, it may not have learnt how to control their shift yet. And if they haven't had somebody to guide them, they can go insane from the power, especially if it's a bitten.'

The black wolf came so quickly and suddenly that I didn't expect it. One moment I was talking and the next I was being landed on. I rolled with it, ending up on top of Erik.

'What the hell Erik?' I said.

We heard the obvious click of a gun. 'Get off him.' I did as Colby instructed. The wolf was on the ground between us.

'Tell me why I shouldn't shoot you?' Colby said. The wolf got to his feet, tail raised. He growled. 'You can't get all dominant on me, you're not my alpha. She is.' He clicked the safety off when the black wolf growled. 'Why do you think I volunteered to teach her in the first place?'

The wolf growled again. 'You know you can't beat me in a fight.' Colby snarled in response, it was the snarl more than the words that shocked me. 'Get lost.'

I had never seen Erik back down. He seemed to growl in frustration before running back the way he came. 'I think tonight's run will be good for you,' I commented. He was tense, Colby was usually the calm and collected one. 'Should I send any vamp attacks your way next time?'

'Very funny.' he stated drily. I smirked.

'Did you even have the right bullets?' I asked him.

'Nope.' He grinned as he put the safety back on and slipped the glock into the back of his jeans before covering it with his shirt.

I rolled my eyes. 'You really are asking for it.'

'It's been quiet lately. Leave me alone.'

I just grinned and turned to leave. I paused. I'd completely forgotten about the human crowd and judging by the look on Colby's face he had too. 'I'm gonna get some rest before tonight,' I told Colby. 'I'm still recuperating after yesterday.'

'Yeah. I'm going to go for that run and then do the same.' By run he meant hunt. It just avoided the awkwardness when around humans. We walked off in different directions. Colby towards the hunting grounds and me towards my house.

The next day I turned up to school with next to no sleep. The night had seen no action at all, meaning it was a boring night of running around in circles, and passing Colby every five minutes. It didn't seem to help Colby either. He needed a proper fight to take the edge off. He was past the point of running it off.

After a few days of nothing we slowed down on patrols. All six of us were exhausted trying to fit an eight-hour run around our human commitments. Instead we each did a few laps around the perimeter at a certain time of the day, meaning that we would catch anything out of the ordinary.

There had also been no sign of Erik since he backed down to Colby. Toby thought that was amusing since Colby was half his age. After the hard few days ended I started spending more time with Zac.

He knew that I couldn't promise to tell him everything, but I could promise not to lie to him anymore. That, I was okay with. We both had Saturday night free thanks to no more patrols and there being two weeks between games this time. It gave the finalists time to prep for the game. So we went out.

We didn't go anywhere near Kraze, as we would be bombarded with classmates and neither of us wanted that. Instead I took him through the forest. He was worried at first going in at night, but he quickly relaxed when I took his hand and led him into the deeper woods.

I did warn him to stay quiet. 'Where are we going?' he asked when we were almost there.

I shushed him quietly. 'This is the part of the forest where bears and mountain lions live,' I whispered just loud enough for him to hear.

'Then what are we doing out here?'

'We're almost there.'

Despite me not telling him anything he continued to follow me through the trees. Then the trees stopped, opening up onto a rocky clearing. It slanted upwards. It would be difficult to climb. I ignored the wall and walked in a diagonal direction.

'Now stay quiet and don't make any sudden moves,' I warned him. 'Not until they accept you.'

I jumped down onto a hidden ledge, I turned around and helped Zac find his footing without falling off the side. If he did it would be a steep fall. There was an entrance into the stone wall. I ducked my head and walked through.

After several metres, the tunnel opened up into a large cave. At the back was a spring of fresh water. I could sense Zac's awe at the sight of the resting wolf pack. A large grey wolf got to his feet and trotted over to us.

'Hey Ruddy,' I said to the wolf.

'Who's the two legger?' the alpha asked.

'He's a friend of mine,' I stated. 'Don't worry he's safe.'

'Are these werewolves?' Zac asked me, looking around at the dozen canines.

I shook my head. 'They're actual wolves.' I crouched down next to Ruddy. 'Crouch down slowly,' I told him. 'Ruddy is the alpha here. If he accepts you then the rest will too.'

Zac did as I asked. 'Now you don't look in his eyes,' I warned. 'That's a challenge to his leadership.'

Zac looked down, he held himself tensely as the wolf stepped forward and started to sniff the human in his den.

After a moment Ruddy looked at me. *'I'm going to take your word for it,'* he stated.

'Thanks,' I said. 'You guys can go hunt if you want, we'll keep an eye on the pups.'

At the word hunt, every wolf head was raised. Hunting meant food, something that they had trouble finding with pups in tow. 'I picked up a fresh trail of a herd of deer two miles back,' I offered. 'If you follow my trail you should be able to find them.'

Without another word, the wolves disappeared one by one. They were eager to hunt as a pack. 'They listen to you?' Zac questioned.

'They respect me,' I responded. 'We share this land. They stay away from the livestock and we leave this area for them to live in peace.'

I turned away from Zac as three fur balls came bolting towards me. They were about the size of a small dog. I crouched down. 'Hey guys,' I said.

'Rya!' they all screamed into my head at once.

I rubbed my temple. 'You three really need to work on the volume.' They sat, looking sheepish. 'You guys are so big already. You're talking and everything.'

I could sense Zac's amusement. I looked up at him, eyebrow raised questioningly. 'Do you come out here often?' he asked me.

'I try and help out during pup season,' I admitted. 'The pack gets to go hunting and the kids are safe.' I got to my feet as the little wolves ran towards the spring. I knew their bed was over there near the back wall, safe from any intruders.

I followed them and Zac followed me. I cupped water in my hand and drank it. Zac pulled a face. 'This will be the best water you'll find,' I said in response. 'It's clean and pure from the mountain and it runs down through the forest.'

By the time the wolves returned from their hunt I had built a small fire in the centre of the cave. The pups were sitting near the edge mesmerised by the flames. The pack didn't return empty handed. They couldn't get an entire deer into the cave, but they could bring pieces. Several legs were brought back, they usually had the best meat.

Ruddy had a particularly large one. Which he set down in front of me. It was tempting. I saw another wolf nudge the pups, breaking them out of their daze and showing them the food. 'Thanks Rudd,' I said. He put it on the ground skin down so the bare flesh didn't touch the ground.

I picked it up and used my claws to slice off a chunk of meat. I held it over the flames, close enough to cook it quickly but not so close to char it. When that end was cooked I turned it over in my hand and let the other side cook. At least the heat didn't do more then scald my skin.

Zac had remained silent throughout the entire thing. He cringed when I held the meat out to him. 'Try it.' I prompted.

Hesitantly he took it. I took another piece off the bone, this I didn't cook, it tasted better that way. Zac still hadn't eaten the venison. 'It's not going to hurt you,' I promised.

Cautiously he took a bite. I could tell instantly that he was surprised by it. He liked it. I took off a bigger piece as he took another bite, I ate this before he finished what he had. Then I cooked him another bit. He ate that too.

The pack settled around the heat the fire gave them. I didn't really feel it, but we were still coming out of winter. The warmth was appreciated by the wolves. When Zac and I were full there was still a decent amount of meat left.

'You're not eating?' Ruddy asked when I gave the rest to the three kids and they carried it away together.

'I ate yesterday,' I told him, moving to wash my hands in the spring. 'I won't need a big meal for a few more days.'

When I sat back against the cave wall next to Zac he wrapped his arm around my back. 'Thanks for bringing me up here.'

I felt a smile on my face. 'I'm glad you liked it,' I said. 'The others don't see the point in coming out here.'

'Besides the three-hour hike,' Zac commented.

I laughed. 'It doesn't take that long when you're a

werewolf.'

'So we blame the human.'

'Yep.'

Ruddy walked over and laid down beside me. Resting his head on my lap. I put my hand on the back of his neck, scratching his ear just a little. 'I like it out here because it's peaceful,' I admitted.

One by one the wolves drifted closer, settling in for the night after a good meal. They were content. A few of them eyed Zac warily, but they trusted me, and they knew I trusted him. Otherwise I wouldn't have brought him here.

I answered several of Zac's questions about werewolves, wolves and the supernatural. But soon we were both nodding off to sleep. The wolves had left enough room for us to lay down amongst them. I did just that. Using Ruddy's body as a pillow. His head was now on Mura, his mate, as she curled herself around him.

I could sense Zac's feeling of unease. He was worried about the wolves. I rolled over onto my stomach. I was right next to him, our bodies touching. I rested my chin on his chest as he looked down at me. 'It's okay,' I told him. 'The wolves won't hurt you.'

He wrapped his arm around me stopping me from moving away. I didn't care, I was happy where I was. Instead I made myself more comfortable. After a few moments, he started to relax. The last thing I heard before falling asleep was the rhythmic thumping of his heart.

The days leading up to the full moon went quickly, Zac and I spent most of our time together after our trip to the wolf den, he hadn't told anybody about the trip and neither had I. I was glad that we were at the point where we didn't tell our friends where we were going.

In the lead up to the full moon I spent time training both Maya and Mira, getting them ready for the full moon gathering. I hadn't seen any sign of Erik since Colby shut him down. I was glad, he seemed to be keeping a low profile and that meant he wasn't going after me.

I was glad that the full moon was on the weekend. Being the first one where the town knew about us, school would have involved a lot of watching. A lot of humans seeing how we took the day. Since, according to humans, it was the worst time to be living in a town full of werewolves.

On the morning of the full moon I woke up to Zac moving off the bed, I could tell by the position of the rooms light that it was at least mid-morning. He went into the bathroom. I rolled over and stretched before getting to my feet. It was kind of funny how Zac seemed to become comfortable here. He even had some clothes in the cupboard.

I walked silently out of the room and into the kitchen. Zac had made breakfast the last few days. Somehow it was surprising to me that he could actually cook. It just didn't seem like something he would do. I was determined to cook. Except my culinary skills consisted of frying red meat and bacon, and occasionally an egg or two.

When he found me in the kitchen I was already cooking everything that I could. Except for steak, well I cooked one for Zac, mine was raw of course. He couldn't help himself either. He flipped the bacon over to cook the other side.

'No,' I protested. 'I'll do it.'

He grabbed my hand. 'Go,' he ordered. 'Sit.'

'Bu…' I stopped. The look on his face told me that I wouldn't win. Besides, my mind was more focused on his hand. In the end I did what he said and sat down at the table. There I watched as he finished what I started.

We talked about random things. Mostly the upcoming game tonight. Was it strange that neither of us brought up the full moon tonight? The fact that I would have to leave during the game. I hated it, but unfortunately it couldn't be helped. At least Zac managed to convince his team to throw the victory party next weekend, if they did win.

I did the dishes, in return for breakfast but as always, Zac was determined to do something. I don't know why but it felt like he was trying to prove himself. I was putting the plates away when I turned around and bumped into him.

I stopped the plates from falling but once again my wolf was buzzing from the touch. I hated full moons for this reason. Judging by the look on Zac's face he'd felt it too. I put the plates away to avoid looking at him. This was my wolf doing this to us. I tended to avoid Zac on full moons.

But Zac didn't let me escape. He grabbed my hand and pulled me towards him before I could disappear into the bathroom. My wolf responded, forcing my body to respond when I really should have pulled away.

I leaned against the bench behind me for support as I wrapped my hand around the back of Zac's neck. I could feel his grin as his lips moved down my neck, I bit my lip to keep from making noise. I knew Zac could sense what he was doing to me, my wolf made sure of that.

Almost by themselves, my hands went up Zac's body, each of his muscles tensing slightly under my touch. Today, his shirt was a button down. So when his lips were back on mine, my hands slowly undid them.

When they were undone he shrugged it off with a grin. He didn't need to prod me. I knew he wouldn't anyway. I pulled my shirt over my head, then I pulled his lips back to mine as it slipped out of my hand and onto the floor. My body moved with his as he urged us back to my room. I should have protested, but I didn't. I gave in.

***

'That…' Zac started, 'was unexpected.'

His arm was wrapped around me, cradling me against him, under the blanket. I rolled over, so my chin rested on his naked chest. 'Side effect of the full moon,' I admitted.

He looked down at me. 'Really?' I nodded. 'I should stay over on full moons more often.' I couldn't stop the smile from stretching across my face.

Zac moved so fast that even I didn't follow him. But one moment we were resting and the next I was on my back and he leaned in to kiss me. I could feel the grin on my face as I wrapped my hand around his neck. His hand ran up the muscles on my stomach until it rested at the base of my ribs.

'Really,' a voice said, and like two kids caught behind the bleachers we broke apart. 'You two couldn't keep it together.'

I knew it was Agua from her voice. But when I turned over I wasn't expecting to see Sean and Dylan behind her. I was so glad the blanket was over me, and judging by the emotion I was sensing from Zac he was too. I pulled the blanket up to cover my naked chest, my bra was on the floor, near the window.

'You mind?' I said. Zac had gone fully embarrassed. The complete opposite of a few moments ago.

Agua seemed to get the message. She grabbed the handle and shut the door. I rolled over and faced Zac. 'Where exactly did we leave our shirts?' he asked me, an embarrassed smile on his face.

'I think they're on the kitchen floor.'

'Oh my god.' He buried his face in the pillow.

'Don't worry,' I said moving closer. 'Agua doesn't care. The most she'll do is joke about it later.'

'I'm not talking about Agua.' He turned his face to look at me his brown eyes bore into my yellow ones. 'I thought we wanted to keep our relationship private,' he said.

'We do,' I agreed. 'But in this town, that won't really happen, especially since it's full of werewolves.' I kissed him softly. 'We'd better get out there before Agua comes back.'

He raised an eyebrow. 'She'd do that?'

'Hell yeah.' He laughed at my response.

I climbed out of the bed and walked into my cupboard. I could feel Zac watching as I pulled clean clothes on. Fully dressed, I went to the door. 'You coming?' I questioned. Zac still hadn't moved.

'I'm considering crawling under the bed.'

'Pick up all the clothes while you're at it.' I caught sight of the smirk before I closed the door behind me. A moment later I heard him get out of bed.

I didn't go straight to the lounge, I ducked into the kitchen and grabbed the two shirts off the floor without being spotted. I tossed them onto the bed. By this time Zac was dressed and he followed me out.

I tried my best to focus on something other than him walking behind me. *Seriously.* I thought to my wolf. *Cut it out.*

They all looked our way when we entered the lounge. When I sat on the couch Zac sat next to me. His arm resting across the cushion behind me. Agua was the one that spoke first. 'Nice to see you with clothes on,' she commented.

'Leave it alone Agua,' I said, glaring at my friend slightly.

'Erik's is going to hate you for this,' she commented.

'He already hates me,' I responded. 'This won't make much of a difference.'

Dylan looked suddenly curious. 'Why would this

make a difference with Erik?'

I cut across Agua before she could speak. 'Let's talk about something else,' I put in. 'Like the reason you all came here.'

'They were looking for Zac,' Agua stated. 'I told them he was over here.'

'What's up?' Zac asked them. I could feel his awkwardness.

'You missed training.' Sean stated.

'Really?' Zac seemed surprised. 'What time is it?'

'It's three.' Dylan stated.

Really? I glanced at the clock, sure enough time was just ticking over the three o'clock mark. Everyone looked at me. 'Hey, this isn't my fault,' I said defensively. Okay, it kind of was but seriously. 'You should go with them,' I told Zac.

'Are you coming?' he asked.

'Yeah,' I responded. 'I just have to get a few things organised before tonight.' A few minutes later Zac was walking out the door with his friends.

***

I was almost relieved when the other team arrived. It meant that the game would start soon. I got to my feet and walked up to our team.

'You okay?' Zac asked me, he touched a comforting hand to my arm.

'Yeah,' I stated. 'It's just a matter of resisting for a while longer.'

'And if you don't,' Jace questioned.

'If we were any danger we wouldn't be here,' I told him. 'We just... don't worry. It's too difficult to explain and right now I can't focus on much more than staying human.'

'You don't have to stay,' Zac said, touching his hand to my arm.

'Yes, I do,' I responded. 'It's not moonrise for another hour.'

'Is this going to be like the other week?' Zac asked.

'No,' I told him. 'The opposite actually.'

'What happened the other week?' Dylan asked.

'Best you don't know,' I told him.

I walked back to my friends when the coach walked towards the team. Sitting under this tree we were close enough to the field to see and hear everything. But we were also fairly close to the forest. Which meant we could easily slip away when it was time.

When kick off finally came, our team started with the ball after the usual coin toss. Zac and Dylan up the front, our forwards or strikers if you wanted to call them that. We watched as much of the game as I thought we could stand. 'Let's go,' I told the other two. Maya would already be heading to the meeting place; I'd shown her where to go the other day.

It was then that something shot out of the trees at the other end of the field. It had to be more than one. When the first one that had appeared grabbed one of the opposing team I moved. So did Toby and Mira. They were right behind me.

That was when the others appeared. 'Let him go,' I half growled at the vamp.

'Shouldn't you wolfies be on your mountain?' he asked.

The resounding crack of Mira's bone confirmed what he said. 'Mira go,' I stated. 'Your mother will be waiting for you.' She didn't get to; we were surrounded. Six of them. 'Ready to put your training to the test?' I asked Toby, he didn't respond, he was struggling to stay on two legs.

'Let the human go,' I told the vampire.

'How about no,' he responded.

The three of us stood back to back. Mira had no way to escape. Why did she follow us over? There was a stalemate. Until the vampire in front of me caught fire. The source didn't take long to find. Agua. Her hand was stretched out in front of her. The vampire yelled for the briefest moment before he burst into ash.

'Good one,' I said, then all of us moved. The human scrambled away from the smoking ash at his feet.

I attacked the one closest to me, ducking under his arm and shoving him into his neighbour. Within moments they were both dead. Three down, three to go. Several cracks announced Mira's transformation taking over her. She hunched over, trying her best not to whimper.

Toby was fighting one, but he was also holding back the moon's pull. I could tell because he kept hunching over and forcing himself to stand up straight. The remaining two went after Mira. She was already on the ground, half way to wolf, vulnerable. Not as painful as the dark moon, but still painful, because it was her first time.

I leaped at one of them. I landed on top of her, leaning over the vampire like I was about to rip out its throat. I could have done it too. Instead I used my hands. I saw Toby collapse as he started to change. 'Come on Toby stay human for me,' I said, but it was no use his skin was already being replaced by fur.

I grimaced as my own wolf tried to force me to change. Come on girl, there's two left. Agua blasted the vampire away from Toby. It landed several metres away and seconds later it burst into flames. I turned to attack the last vampire but stopped.

'This is your human, isn't it?' she asked. 'He smells like you. I have to say, I like your taste. His blood smells sweet.'

My lip curled, I held back the snarl. 'Mira, Toby.' They both lifted their heads, ears flicking forward as they looked at me. 'Go.' I coiled my muscles against the next tremor. They both got to their feet and ran off into the trees.

'I'm surprised you're still standing kid,' she sneered.

'I'm not exactly new at this,' I told her. 'They are.' I felt my arm snap. I grimaced. It wasn't supposed to hurt, but I had held it in.

'But you can't hold it back for long.' She wore a smirk. My body tried to double over. I forced myself to stay on two legs. My vision changed, I shook away my wolf eyes. I had moments. I glanced behind me the sun had set, now only the large moon was staring down at me.

My eyes met Zac's for the briefest of moments. I knew that he understood my intentions. I twitched slightly. He broke his arm free and elbowed the bitch in the face. He broke out of her grip at the same time that I leapt forward.

Now I let my skin melt, the transformation coming fast and smooth. By the time I landed on the vampire, I was a full wolf. I stood over her, a growl rumbling in the back of my throat. She seemed shocked. That was the last expression she wore before I used my newly grown fangs to rip out her dead throat.

She disintegrated under my feet as I shook out my fur. I glanced at Zac. He was staring at me, but didn't look shocked or surprised. He had known what I was going to do. I brushed past him, my fur touching his leg. I felt his hand touch the back of my ear for the briefest of moments. Then I bolted into the trees.

It didn't take me long to reach the pack. Not on four legs. *'You're late,'* Erik growled upon seeing me.

'Vamp attack,' I stated easily, he would be able to smell them anyway. *'We were about to leave when they came.'*

'Whatever. Enough time has been wasted already.' Time, huh, we had all night and weren't doing anything but hunting and sleeping.

Erik raised his head, releasing a loud howl that vibrated off the trees. The rest of the pack followed only moments later. We were here and we were on the hunt. We were already moving before the pack sound left the forest eerie and silent.

When I woke up I was naked, I always was. It was a normal part of the full moon night, if you could call waking up in the middle of the forest surrounded by naked people normal. I lifted my head up off the ground. It pounded, a side-effect of the adrenaline from the night before, we were always like this after a full moon.

I got up silently and went to the small shelter, grabbing a set of clothes from one of the bags and pulled them on. Hopefully I could get away before Erik noticed, Zac was meeting me for breakfast and I really wanted to know if they won.

I probably got a mile away from the den before he caught up. That wasn't hard, my head was throbbing too badly to run. He pinned me easily to the ground. I couldn't even fight him off, he knew it too. He was human within seconds.

'Erik.' I could hear the fear in my own voice.

Erik leaned into my throat. He put his hands down my shorts. Both pulling them down and pulling me closer to him. There was no point fighting him. He stopped, his nose on my neck. Inhaling the scent on my skin he growled. 'What have you done?' His voice was low and threatening.

Then he was gone. I took a deep shaky breath. I

realised what direction he'd gone in. I got to my feet and bolted towards the human world. Somehow I managed to reach Erik before he could do anything to the waiting Zac.

Zac was backing away as Erik slowly stepped towards him. I slid in between them. 'Erik stop,' I said. I was crouched on the ground, ready to attack. But even I could hear the slightest hint of begging in my voice.

'You're mine,' he growled. 'This human has contaminated you.'

'I was never yours,' I snarled in response. 'I was a child that you took advantage of every time you had an itch.'

He leapt at me. I rolled with him and ended up on top, but with my foggy head I didn't stay there. He bit my arm with exposed fangs and flipped us back over. I let out a shaky breath as the pain of the bite washed through me. He stepped towards Zac again.

My wolf rose with anger, forcing me to get up, I blinked and she was staring out of my eyes. I dove for Erik, hitting him in the side. He lost grip on his wolf form and he rolled another metre as a human. He looked at me once he had stopped.

'Touch him, and I won't stop until I rip your throat out,' I growled.

My mind was clear now. Thanks to the wolf that stared out of me. I knew that if I transformed now, I would be gone. Erik smirked, he knew. My back was to the forest, so I didn't see the wolves that came walking out of the forest, not until they were beside me.

Hackles were raised, snarls ready to go. They were my pack. One of them, Colby, went and stood protectively in front of Zac. Erik was looking around, he might have been hoping they would side with him.

'What is this?' Erik growled.

I felt the sneer on my face. 'Zac is mine,' I growled. 'If you kill him, you'll be breaking every one of our laws. I won't have to be strong enough to kill you, because they'll do it.'

A snarl ripped out of Colby's throat. 'Now get out of here,' he growled.

At first Erik didn't move but then Colby stepped towards him. The naked werewolf moved pretty quickly after that. Within seconds he had become a wolf and was bolting into the forest, the pack parting for him as he ran.

My wolf wanted to go after him, the human part of me stopped us. That would only start a fight I knew we couldn't win. I sensed Colby walk up to me. He nuzzled into my neck with his cold, wet nose.

I couldn't help but grin. 'I'm fine,' I told the wolf, my hand scratching him once behind the ear. 'But I could use a shower and several days of sleep.'

The wolf huffed with laughter, pushing me over with his snout. 'Hey,' I complained from where I now sat. I dove at him playfully, I pinned him to the grass a moment later I released him. I looked up at the rest of the wolves. They all wore expressions of amusement. I nodded once. Before they turned around and disappeared back into the forest. I looked at Zac.

'So did you win?' I asked.

**

Word about the altercation spread like wildfire

through the smallish town. Also the fact that Zac was the cause also spread. The soccer team win wasn't big news anymore. We didn't end up going to breakfast. Instead we went back to the house where I could get rid of the feeling of Erik on me.

I was glad that Zac didn't say anything about what I said. Even I couldn't really believe that I said it. The fact that I claimed him. In the world of werewolves that was a big thing. It was against pack law to kill a human that was claimed by another werewolf. Unless of course they were a danger.

But Zac had also found out the full extent of Erik's abuse. The whole town had. I didn't know if I was ready for them to see me that way. As a victim, damaged. I had worked so hard since becoming a werewolf to make sure I was strong. Pity was the last thing I wanted.

For the first time for a week, that night I slept alone. I had gone to sleep after having a long hot shower. And when I had awoken, Zac hadn't been there. I assumed that he went home, or gone to Dylan or Sean's. I didn't blame him.

But when he didn't turn up for school on Monday morning I grew worried. By the end of the day I had spoken to just about everyone, including Alec. Nobody had seen him since Sunday morning.

At that point I called Colby. He wrangled together as many police and pack members that he could. Together we scoured the entire town. Every scent we found was old. His scent had been covered to stop us from finding him. Where was he?

ZAC HALL

'What do you want?' I whimpered through gritted teeth.

Erik pulled his hand back, his protruding claws were covered in blood, my blood. 'You took everything from me,' he growled. 'You and your father both. He took our secrecy. You, you took my pack, you took Rya from me. So I'm going to make both of them suffer,' he continued. 'Killing you is the key to that.' I should have been terrified. I should be; but I wasn't. I was just angry.

He turned around and left the dark room. No light could enter unless the door was open. I moved to the corner of the small room. I had just settled with my back to the wall when the door opened again.

I caught a brief glimpse of Erik as he threw something into the room with me. The door closed again before I could see what it was. From the direction of the thump came a small whine. I wasn't alone.

RYA GARCIA

I ignored the fact that Alec was watching us. At least I tried to ignore it. Finally I sighed and pulled my shirt over my head as I let my skin slide, fur sprouting all over my body. Toby was only a few beats behind me. Colby was staying human

Colby nodded his head in the direction we needed to go. I nodded, telling him to lead the way. We took off, running deeper into the forest at full speed, leaving Alec to stand at the fringe of the trees with Agua and Dylan.

We had decided to check the various structures out in the forests. The first stop on our list was Erik's since it was the closest, and the fact that Erik could very well have taken Zac to punish us for Sunday. It didn't take us long to reach the outskirts of town, the place in question was an old house on a small piece of land, it had a stone basement strong enough to hold an ordinary werewolf on the dark moon, it wasn't strong enough to hold me.

There was no point sneaking up, Erik would hear us coming. So instead we took the direct approach. I could smell him, I knew he was nearby, the scent was fresh. I could even smell Zac, there was also another scent, one I recognised, the rogue wolf that killed that boy.

A growl rumbled in my throat as I walked cautiously towards the rundown looking house. I was closely followed by an equally cautious Colby and Toby. *'Go get Zac,'* I told them. They walked past me towards the house, they slipped silently over the broken threshold.

ZAC HALL

The person moved. 'Who are you?' I asked quietly, trying not to startle the person.

The shadow moved so quickly. 'Why did he do this to this one?' a girl's voice whimpered. 'He locked me in here with a *human*,' she rambled. 'Humans are dangerous, he said.' The voice came from the corner. 'They will kill this one, he said. That's why this one hides.'

She must be a werewolf. 'It's okay,' I said, moving closer.

The shadow flinched. 'It's trying to lure this one in,' the girl said. 'Pretending to be nice. It's going to kill this one. It doesn't know what this one is capable of. This one can hurt him if this one wants to. He would let this one. He would be proud of this one. This one wants to please him.'

I moved a little closer. I wasn't sure how smart that was, this girl was obviously crazy. What had Erik done to her? 'Who are you?' I asked again.

'This one has no name,' she answered. 'This one shouldn't talk to the human. This one should kill the human, make him proud. But this one doesn't want to kill. The urge is strong in this one, the power within wants to kill, she wants blood, she wants death. Should this one give in?' she continued to mutter to herself, arguing with herself. 'This one wants blood,' the girl stated suddenly. 'Blood will ease the hunger.' I backed away as a growl came from the corner the room.

RYA GARCIA

I growled. *'What did you do to him?'* The moment the others had entered the house Erik had appeared.

'Nothing that won't heal,' Erik sneered in reply.

I could hear the sounds of a fight inside the house. *'Who's with you?'*

The black wolf didn't answer, instead it attacked. I rolled to the side, out of reach. I was on my feet a moment later, spinning on the spot to turn around and grab at Erik. My teeth sank into the flesh of his hind leg.

I crunched my teeth, I felt the skin break under my canines, blood splattered into my mouth as I crushed bone. I felt the growl of pain vibrate through Erik. Just before he lashed out, he grabbed me by the throat and threw me. I hit a tree. Too crowded. The wolf told me. Need more room. The words broke through the link to my wolf and for once, I listened. I got to my feet dodging out of Erik's reach, then I started running, Erik close on my heels.

TOBY DAVIS

We reached the door to the basement, we could hear the growls on the other side, something was in there with Zac. Colby quietly opened the door. I bolted through it the second it opened, standing between Zac and a small dark coloured wolf.

I growled at the wolf. I could hear Colby grabbing Zac and taking him out of the room. They weren't quick enough, I wasn't quick enough. The wolf leaped at Zac, forcing him to the ground with its weight. I didn't think, I dove.

AGUA FRAY

The moment I heard about Erik and Rya, I bolted out of the house, I ran for the park. What were they even doing there? The house was ages away from the park? When I arrived, they were wrestling, both of them trying to gain the advantage. Blood stained the white fur around Rya's mouth, Erik was limping slightly.

I pushed past the startled humans towards the fight. By the time I reached the front Rya had been flung, she hit the ground and rolled, I heard bone break. I sensed it as the humans winced at the sound. Rya didn't get back up. She turned back into human form, and she remained face down in the grass, she was covered in blood.

Erik walked towards his fallen opponent, but still she didn't move. Was she alive? I couldn't tell. The black wolf looked pleased with himself as he looked down upon Rya. *Come on Rya, get up*.

RYA GARCIA

Now! I reacted. I leaped at the wolf that stood above me. My teeth extended as I closed my still human jaw around his throat. My teeth closed around his windpipe, I tasted the blood that flowed freely into my mouth. A growl resonated within my chest as the black wolf stopped moving. Erik was already turning human by the time he hit the ground. His face frozen in shock as I ripped the life out of him.

I could feel the blood in my throat arousing the

wolf that was already so close to the surface. I had started the transformation. I took a deep breath. Wolf pushed on the walls of her cage. She wanted more blood. I could feel my canines protruding from my mouth, my claws were extending out of my fingers.

I gripped the ground, my claws digging into the earth, holding me steady. Wolf was growing stronger the longer that the blood was in my system. My breaths came short and jagged as I tried to settle her.

I saw it as my face slowly and painfully stretched to form a muzzle. I whimpered in pain when my already broken bone snapped. I crouched on the ground trying to pull the wolf back into the human. I forced myself to take long deep breaths, but I couldn't stop the cry of pain as my spine curled.

It was a battle of the minds, each of us trying to take control of the body, the human against the wolf. It was like a never-ending wrestling match. I had never imagined it to be so painful, but then I had never gone so far and come back before.

Stopping the wolf from taking control resulted in my muzzle sinking once again back into a mouth and nose. The fur that had begun to grow sank back under my skin, leaving my skin raw and numb. My bones snapped painfully back into place, and I held in a cry of pain when my arm broke for the third time.

When the wolf finally let me go, I was human again. If I hadn't have been crouching on the ground I would have fallen over. As it was I had to catch myself, using my trembling hand to hold myself up.

My body heaved in large gulps of air. Then without warning my body forced Erik's blood out of my system. I gulped as I tried to push myself to my feet. My legs collapsed below me, forcing me back to all fours. My vision faded as dizziness overcame my senses. The last thing I saw was Colby running out of the forest towards me.

I was alone when I woke up. My broken arm had healed, so had the claw marks. The only evidence of the fight were the bruises that covered my abdomen. I looked around, taking in my surroundings. I was in my room. Slowly I forced myself into a sitting position. My head spun slightly. I shook my head to clear it.

I forced myself to climb out of bed and walk into the bathroom. What I saw in the mirror was a bloody mess. Though somebody had put clothes on me and probably tried to clean the wounds, they still left blood behind.

It took one extremely long shower and several hair washes to get rid of it all. After I was clean I had just sat in the bottom under the steaming, hot water. My skin was red raw from the scalding, but I didn't care.

'Rya?' I looked up, startled by the voice. Colby.

'Hey.' My voice cracked. 'How long was I out?'

'Three days.' I was too tired to respond to the length of my recovery period. 'You didn't start healing till yesterday,' Colby continued in my absence of speech.

'Where's Zac?' I asked, suddenly remembering the

reason for the showdown with Erik.

'He's resting in the other room,' the werewolf said. 'He's safe.'

I got to my feet and shut off the water. Colby handed me a towel. I dried off and went to my cupboard for some clothes. I grabbed basic moon clothes knowing I would have to hunt anyway. I could feel the hunger starting to grip my stomach.

I went through the house to the room where I could hear somebody breathing. 'Rya.' Colby stopped me at the door. 'There's something you should know.'

'What?' I asked.

'Zac was bitten,' he stated; I froze. 'Erik had a young female locked in his basement. We didn't get there in time to stop her.'

I took a deep breath. 'Leave me.' My voice was small.

'Ry...'

'Leave me.' My voice was more forceful this time. He ducked his head and left. A moment later I heard the front door open and close.

When I opened the door, there was no denying Colby's claim. I could smell the sickness caused by the bite all over the room. It would be over by now though. It usually only took two days to get through it.

I closed the door silently behind me and walked over to the bed. Zac was curled up in a ball under the blanket. He was awake, but right now everything would be overwhelming the sights, the smells, the sounds, everything. It would be too much to take in at once.

When I moved onto the bed, he turned over, looking at me with golden yellow eyes. It didn't look right. He didn't look right with werewolf eyes. I took a deep breath; even his scent had changed.

I laid down on the bed beside him. This new Zac was going to take a while to get used to. After a moment, he moved closer and wrapped me in his comforting arms, his body pressed against my back. I felt the touch of his lips on the top of my head; his way of reassuring me he was still him… for now at least.

'They told me that you did it,' Zac said after several minutes of silence. 'That you killed him.'

'Yeah,' I admitted. 'I did.'

'How did it feel to take him down?'

'I don't know,' I said. 'I nearly jumped off the edge to take him down. I let too much wolf in and she nearly claimed me.'

He was silent for a moment. 'What you said the other day…' he stopped, 'what did it mean?'

'You mean the thing that started this whole mess?' I questioned. I felt his smirk against the back of my neck. 'It's a thing with werewolves,' I explained. 'A werewolf can't kill a human claimed by another werewolf. It's one of our biggest laws.'

'But a claim works both ways,' I continued. 'Erik thought I was his, but I wasn't, I was yours.'

'And that's why he came after me.'

'Yes,' I responded. 'Kill you and the claim is broken.'

'So you didn't just say it to save my skin.'

'That depends on which me you're talking about.' I turned over so I was facing him. 'The human me would never say something like that out loud. It's so… corny.'

He grinned. 'And the wolf you?'

'She wouldn't hesitate.'

He pulled me closer, his nose snuggling into my neck. I felt the grin on my face as I wrapped my hand around his neck and pulled his face up to meet mine. Our lips were just about to touch when my stomach growled audibly.

We both cracked up laughing. 'Guess I'm hungry,' I said. Pulling away from him, he looked like he wanted to protest. 'Come on. I've gotta eat. And you need a shower.'

'Thanks.' He came out of the bed after me.

He did go for a shower. He needed it. The smell of sickness clung to him, even though it had passed now. I waited for him by fixing up the room. It was starting to stink out the rest of the house, I opened the windows wide, changed the bed and turned on the fan.

By the time Zac came out of the bathroom the smell was still there but it wasn't as strong. 'You've been busy,' he commented. I was on my way back into the room at the time.

'I can't stand it,' I admitted. I put the small device on the bedside. It was one of those air freshener type devices. Except this one released a constant mist of the scent, it only lasted an hour and it would make the whole room smell nice again. I would much rather smell that then the sickness caused by a werewolf bite.

'So what are we eating?' Zac asked, following me out of the room.

'I need to hunt,' I admitted. 'You might be transitioning

but your body probably won't accept raw meat yet.'

I took a nicer set of clothes with me in a plastic shopping bag. Zac followed me out of the house and into the forest. He had never seen me hunt before. I could sense vague curiosity coming off of him.

We walked steadily through the trees. I didn't catch sight of any werewolves. In fact the forest was silent except for the creek I could hear in the distance. I stopped, holding my hand up to stop Zac from moving. I silently put the bag of clothes down.

'Stay here,' I told him.

He obeyed as I walked onwards, following the scent of herbivore. I found the herd of deer nestled in a dip in the forest. They were using it to shield them from view, however, it left the vulnerable to attacks from above. Like mine.

I leapt off the rocky ledge. Shifting as I landed on the closest one, a young buck. My weight forced him to the ground. He struggled against me but I quickly closed my teeth around his throat, ending his life quickly and painlessly.

The best thing about quick kills was the lack of mess. At least on me. As I tore into the flesh blood seeped freely from the deer's throat onto the earth below it. I ate my fill then left the rest. The coyotes would finish off the rest, the scavengers. I was able to return to Zac's position with barely a speck of blood on my fur. That speck was around my mouth.

I shifted back into human form when I reached my clothes, still sitting in the bag next to Zac. I quickly pulled the clothes on over my naked skin. Afterwards I stashed the plastic bag into my pocket. 'Now it's time for you to eat,' I stated as I turned towards him.

Zac followed me to the edge of the park. There wasn't really anybody there. I think it was a school day, which meant everyone would be at school and work. That didn't bother me, it meant that we wouldn't have to deal with so many people.

We went into Kraze where Zac ordered a meal, I ordered a bowl of fries. We ignored the people that were staring at us. This was one of those times where I wish I could access human minds. I wanted so badly to know what they were thinking about us.

We had just finished ordering when a group of school students came through the door. School must have finished. It took a moment for Dylan and Sean to notice us. They obviously hadn't been looking for us, but most people scanned a café out of habit when they entered, looking for people they knew.

'Hey.' Dylan seemed a little too excited to see us as he and Sean sat in the seats opposite to us. 'You're finally awake.'

'Yeah,' I said. 'Apparently I was unconscious for three days.'

'Yeah,' Dylan said. 'Everyone's been worried. Colby told us you weren't healing.'

'Apparently,' I responded. 'I don't know, I was in a kind of void.' Everything had been black, in fact it barely felt like more than an hour that I was in there. 'A kind of stasis I couldn't get out of.'

'How often does that kind of thing happen?' Sean asked.

'Not very often.'

'Was it because you stopped yourself from

shifting?' Jace asked, sliding onto the seat next to Zac.

I moved over to make more space. 'I didn't just stop myself from shifting. I stopped myself from losing control. I have never gotten that close and come back before,' I admitted. 'My best guess is when I shut out my wolf I shut out her healing and that caused me to lose consciousness.' I was actually surprised by how reasonable my theory sounded, especially since I hadn't really thought about it.

'What about you?' Dylan was looking at Zac. 'How are you doing?'

He gave a half-hearted shrug. 'Everything is different.'

'How so?' Sean looked curious.

'Everything looks and sounds different. It's…'

'Loud,' I offered. He nodded. 'It takes a while to get used to.'

'It's weird too,' he continued. 'It's like I can feel everyone around me.'

'That's normal too,' I admitted. 'I'll teach you to block it out so it doesn't become too much to handle.'

'It's fine,' Zac said. 'It's not bothering me.'

'It will when you go into a crowded place,' I informed him. 'It's fine here right now, but go to a crowded party and it won't be so easy. And after you turn it can be dangerous.'

'You just woke up.' Toby walked up to the table. 'Shouldn't you be taking it easy.'

'I have a week to prep Zac for the dark moon,' I told him. 'Taking it easy isn't going to work if he's going to survive it.' I gave him a look. 'Unless you want to do it.'

'Hell no,' both Toby and Zac said it at the same time.

I smirked. 'Good to see Zac getting bit didn't change anything.'

'I saved his ass from being torn apart,' Toby stated. 'He should be grateful he's not dead.'

The waitress came out with our food then. She even gave us a small dish of gravy. 'You know chips aren't going to do it for you right?' Toby stated.

'Shut it Toby,' I said. 'I've already eaten.'

He huffed. He glanced at Zac's plate. 'Fish tastes disgusting by the way.' He turned around and left.

I glanced at Zac's plate. I knew what Toby meant, compared to all other meats fish tasted terrible. 'You agree with him.'

I pulled a face. 'I grew up in Agua's house so I eat more food than most werewolves but fish is the one thing I definitely won't eat.' They all grinned. I shrugged. 'I don't know, it's an overkill on the senses.'

Zac just smirked and ate a big piece of fish. I waited. A moment later it looked like he got a sudden burst of adrenaline. 'Whoa,' he said.

'See what I mean.' I was the one grinning now.

'Yeah,' he admitted. 'That tastes different.'

I couldn't help it, I laughed. 'You'll learn what you should and shouldn't eat.'

He wrapped his arm around my shoulder and pulled me closer. I pulled away when he kissed my temple. 'Come on, your breath stinks like fish.'

'There's no pleasing you today is there.'

He squeezed me tighter. I couldn't stop my reaction to the pain the erupted through my body. I actually flinched and pulled back. 'You okay?' I could smell Zac's sudden worry.

'Yeah.' I heard the annoyance in my voice. 'I'm still healing.'

I lift my shirt up to inspect the bruising. I hadn't made the effort to look earlier. 'They look painful,' Dylan commented.

'Yeah.' The bruises looked like green and purple blotches all over my skin.

'That's from the fight?' Jace asked.

'No, I was there,' Sean said. 'Nothing he did could have caused bruises like that.'

'No,' I agreed. 'It was my punishment for pulling back my wolf. They'll take longer to heal,' I admitted. 'But I would rather a few bruises then the alternative.'

'Yeah, we wouldn't want that would we.' I looked at the source of the voice.

'Damien?' There was disbelief in my voice.

'Hey, Sis.' Damien had the normal Garcia blonde hair, solid build and exposed muscles. Obviously he also had the werewolf's golden eyes. All of that I expected. I didn't expect to see the petite female werewolf standing behind him.

The boys leaned back in their seats as I climbed over them. Damien came forward, closing the distance between us. I put my hand up to stop him from hugging me. It worked. He hesitated before stepping back again. I leaned against the table behind me. All attention was on us.

'How long have you been in town?' My voice was guarded. I kept glancing between the two of them.

'A few hours,' he said. 'I went looking for you at home. You changed the locks?'

'What do you want Damien?'

'I saw you on the news,' he said. 'I wanted to make

sure you were okay.'

'As you can see, I'm fine.' I had imagined being happy to see him again, but now I was just bristling with anger. 'You can leave now.'

'What if I don't want to leave?' he said.

'You left me,' I stated. 'I'm sure it wouldn't be too hard to do again.'

'Erik would have killed me if I didn't leave,' he defended. 'I wasn't strong enough to take him down. What was I supposed to do?'

'You should have talked to me.' I knew he could sense my brimming anger. 'I looked everywhere for you. I called everyone. I spent weeks trying to track you.'

'You were safe with Colby,' he stated.

'Our parents had just died,' I spat. 'I watched that thing murder them before he came after me. I barely got away. I didn't need to be safe. I needed my family.'

'Erik gave me till the dark moon to get out of town,' he claimed. 'So I shifted, then I left before you woke up.'

'I wasn't there,' I stated. 'Because I turned that night too. Six years early. I should be just finishing my first year of training like the rest... sorry, like Toby, because Erik killed the rest of us.'

'I didn't know that would happen,' he said. 'I'm sorry.'

'There were fifteen kids before you left, now there's eight, because everyone was afraid that Erik would kill them or their kids, so the pack stopped having kids altogether.'

'I'm sorry,' he repeated.

I stood up fully, crossing my arms. 'I thought I would be okay with it if you ever came back,' I said. 'But I'm not. You can get your stuff and get out of my house.'

'Where am I supposed to go then?' he asked.

'I don't care,' I stated. 'You have to earn back my trust if you want to stay in town, but you're not staying with me.'

'You heard her.' Colby had appeared at the door of the café. 'Leave.'

'Colby?' There was a wounded tone in Damien's voice.

Colby crossed his arms, mirroring my stance. 'We've gone without you for six years. The pack doesn't need you, we have Rya now.'

'Is that the pack's opinion or yours?' Damien glanced between the two of us.

'Both,' Colby responded. 'She could have left us but she didn't. She fought for us, putting herself in the line of fire and stopped Erik from killing us all while you ran away with your tail between your legs.'

'You seem to have grown a lot bolder since I left.' Damien raised an eyebrow.

'None of us are the same as you remember. We had to change or there would be nothing left,' Colby answered.

'You won't get any sympathy here,' I told him. 'You turned your back on us, so we've turned our backs on you.'

'This is my home,' my brother claimed. 'My pack.'

'It's as Rya said. Earn a place or leave,' Colby stated. 'But you'll never be the alpha. Rya has earned that title.'

Our eyes met. The two of us had defied Erik together so many times. He'd helped me get strong enough to defeat him. We had understanding between us, a strong familial bond. 'It's up to you. Just stay out of my way.' Damien turned to look at me. 'I'll organise for your stuff to be moved to an empty pack house.'

I glanced at the small werewolf behind him. 'Now take your girl and get out.'

Damien stared at me for a moment, then he walked towards Colby. The girl stared into my eyes as she started to follow then looked away, but then she turned back to face me when Damien reached the door. 'Why are you treating him like this?' she questioned. 'He's your brother.'

'I don't care if you're from another pack or if you were a victim of the bite, but you're in our territory, so you follow our rules. And in case you haven't noticed, it's up to me if you enter my pack.'

'Come on Sarah.' Damien came back and led her away before she could say anything else. He was the one that paused this time. He looked at Zac. 'I heard what happened to you. I'm sorry,' he said. 'Somebody should have warned you about the danger that follows our family.'

'I think I've worked that out myself,' Zac stated from his seat. 'After all, from what I've been told, I could be dead in a week.'

My brother raised an eyebrow. I could tell he didn't approve. 'You seem to be handling it fairly well, I would expect Alec Hall's son to be as weak minded as the man himself.'

I could have growled, but I didn't. I didn't have to. Colby shoved Damien out the door. 'Get out of here,' the werewolf growled. The female ducked out after my brother, avoiding Colby's gaze. She might not think much of me but she wasn't going to risk crossing Colby.

I leaned up against the table again, my hand gripping my side. Guess I wasn't up to fighting speed yet. It was a wonder I hadn't faltered in front of my brother. 'You okay?' Colby asked me.

'Yeah.' I nodded.

'I didn't come here because of him,' Colby said. 'I came to tell you that the wolf we caught is human now. We managed to trap her in human form, so if we want to talk to her, now's our best chance.'

Wolf? Right… the one that bit Zac. 'Has she said anything?' I asked.

'Nothing coherent. She's speaking Greek.'

I glanced back at Zac, tossing him the keys to the house. For once I had actually locked it. I'm glad, seeing as Damien had made his way back. 'I've got to go translate,' I told him. 'You'll be right to get back?'

He nodded once, he looked like he wanted to come. 'Not this time,' I said before he could get the words out. 'I'll see you when I get back.' I didn't give him the chance to respond as I walked out the door Colby held open.

***

'Who are you?' I asked the girl. She looked maybe ten for a human.

'Please,' she begged, pulling at the manacles that chained her to the wall. 'I just want to go home.'

'You killed a child and turned a human.'

167

'I didn't,' she said. 'I didn't kill that child. He...he used me to cover his scent.' She was speaking fluent Greek. A rare thing for a werewolf these days. 'Please believe me. My name is Amelia. I got separated from my pack when hunters attacked us.'

'Show me.' I stepped closer to her. She shied away. 'It's okay. I'm going to access your memories.' She knelt on the floor in front of me as I put my hand on her head. 'Show me everything.'

It was a mother nuzzling her pup. The pup looked suspiciously like this girl's murky red wolf. After that it was a flood of memories. All of them bad ones. They all hit me at once. It was impossible to sort through them. There were flames and mournful howls of dying wolves.

'Amelia, run,' a woman's voice broke through the image. The mother was running towards the pup yelling out to her as flames flickered to life in the forest surrounding them.

The two wolves ran, racing away from the flames as it licked away the scenery. I flinched as a gunshot rang through my mind. The bullet struck the large wolf, the wolf dropped to the ground, I felt the fear ran through the pup.

The pup's eyes fell onto a man's face. It was shrouded in shadow so it was impossible to tell his identity. The barrel of the gun was pointed towards her. He was just about to pull the trigger when the mother leaped at the man, teeth easily sinking into flesh.

Both of them fell, mother and hunter dropped to the ground, both dead. The dark furred pup trotted to her mother's side as she began to turn back into human form. She nuzzled her mother's face, her ears were flat against her head, tail between her legs.

Then the wolf began to yowl, head raised to the sky, but

nobody answered. She was alone. A flaming tree fell over the top of them, forcing the young wolf to scurry back with a sudden spike of fear. She ran, as fast as she could. She had to get out of the fire. She kept running. She didn't stop.

Alone, tired and hungry, she caught the scent of werewolf. Despite it being another territory, the young wolf walked towards the perimeter. She was past it when fatigue overcame her. She collapsed, her vision fading in and out.

The last thing the small wolf saw was large black wolf walking towards her. The pup whined, softly, silently begging for help. The wolf cautiously sniffed the pup. The little pup tried to get up but she was too weak, collapsing again. Erik, I'm sure it was Erik. Sniffed the pup briefly before picking her up by the scruff as darkness enveloped her.

I came out of the memories gasping for breath. Colby steadied me with a hand, making sure I didn't fall. 'She's telling the truth,' I stated in English. I explained what I saw. 'I think she's from the wild pack.'

'How long ago?' Colby asked.

'I don't know,' I answered. 'Judging by Amelia's size, maybe five.'

'Please let me go,' the girl begged again. 'I didn't mean to bite your human. I couldn't control it.'

I walked closer to her. She flinched when I touched her wrist. She almost looked surprised when I uncuffed her. She rubbed her wrists. I turned to Keith, his eyes staying on the small werewolf in front of us. 'Keith.' He looked at me. 'Take her out to the wild pack. I'm sure they'll be happy to see her.'

'What about the human she killed?' Colby asked

me.

'She didn't do it,' I told him. After seeing her story, I didn't doubt that she had told me the truth. Especially with Erik involved. 'Erik used her to cover up his kill.'

I turned back to the little wolf. 'Keith is going to take you home,' I told her in Greek.

'Thank you.' She seemed to melt.

'Don't thank me,' I stated. 'Just don't let me see you here again.'

Needless to say, the humans weren't happy when they heard I let the werewolf go. To them she was a murderer, to us she was a misled child that got lost and was taken in by a killer. Colby assured them that we had returned her to her own pack and she wouldn't be a problem. They weren't happy about it but they finally accepted it.

I didn't care, I was too busy preparing Zac for the dark moon. That wasn't a very easy thing to do, since I'd never had to deal with a turning human before. I taught him how to use his senses, he learnt how to block things he didn't want to sense. I even helped him strengthen his mind. He would need the extra defence on his mind when the wolf came knocking.

When dark moon day finally came around I thought he was ready. It didn't stop me from being nervous as hell when I woke up. It also didn't help that I knew the entire town would be watching us. They had originally though that the full moon was bad news, now they knew it was actually the dark moon. They really would be watching us now.

I didn't see a single sign of my brother either. I had his stuff moved to another house and he moved into it, him and his girl. I didn't really know how felt about having her here. Despite my reaction the other day, I was kind of glad that he was back.

When I got to school that morning I rested my head on the cool metal of my locker. I took a deep breath. Zac had already gone off to find Dylan and Sean. Mira was sitting on the ground in front of her locker next to Maya, her head in her hands. Even Toby wasn't his usual peppy self. At least Zac wouldn't be feeling this until next month.

Our classmates tiptoed around us all day. We barely spoke, we didn't eat, and if we did we would just throw it up later anyway. We drank only water. When the bell finally rang for the end of the day I was glad to be rid of the glances every time I moved.

Zac wasn't looking too excited when I found him at my locker. Maya was almost curled up against Mira. 'Take her home,' I told Mira. Her family had decided to take Maya in, she had been living with them since the day I killed Erik.

The two girls left in the direction of Maya's new home. Toby and Agua came up to us before I had a chance to talk.

'You three ready?' Agua asked.

None of us answered. Toby just turned around and walked out of the school hallway with the rest of us straggling along behind. We were about to enter the forest when something hit my neck from behind.

I slapped my hand to it. Instantly finding the dart that was sticking out of me. 'Go,' I told the others. 'Go now.' Too late I saw the darts hit them too. Even Agua got one. I stumbled and hit the ground as the sedative pulled me under.

***

'Agua.' My voice had slight panic in it. We were trapped in a cage in the middle of town. Hall and his lackey seemed to have decided to put on a show. She was still out cold from her tranq.

They'd taken all of our phones too. I smashed my shoulder against the bars of the cage, but they were made of solid iron. They weren't moving. I'd been striking the same one repeatedly hoping it would finally budge. All I had to show for it was a red shoulder.

Toby was pacing, his arms crossed, hugging his claws. Zac was sitting in the corner. He had woken up, seen his father and hadn't really moved since. I could only sense the anger that was bristling within him. This was not the best way to become a werewolf.

The sun was setting rapidly. We had maybe twenty minutes before moonrise. I couldn't even call anyone, everybody would be in the process of locking themselves away.

'Hall!' I shouted across the space between us. I sensed Toby stop behind me. Hall looked over at me. 'What are you trying to prove? The world already knows about us.'

'To prove that you're monsters,' he said. 'Tonight will prove that.'

'What happened to our agreement?' My voice was breathless, like I'd been running.

'You didn't keep your end of the bargain,' he responded.

'I said I would talk to you,' I stated. 'There hasn't been time.'

'Ah, wolfies in a cage,' a voice drawled from the

tree line. 'Just how I like them.'

'Alec,' I said. 'Let us out. Now!' Anger brimmed within me as the three vampires came into view.

Reluctantly he obliged, realising the danger instantly. 'Toby, take Zac and go.'

'But what about you?' Toby asked.

'Just go. Now.' There was the hint of an order in my voice.

Without another word the two boys ran towards the house. They should get there in time. No, they had to get there in time.

'Brave little wolfie staying out past her bed time.'

I stalked towards them. I didn't have time for games tonight. I stopped just short of them. They waited ready to strike the moment I did. In the end they attacked first. The first one was stupid enough to come head on. I grabbed her easily by the throat, my hand squeezing her throat until she burst.

The wolf in me bristled, it was almost time and we were free. A second one burst into flames. I sighed with relief Agua was awake. My relief was short lived. The third one attacked me, just as the sun disappeared.

The wolf rammed towards me full throttle. She hit me so hard that I collapsed. It had been a long time since I fought the wolf on a dark moon. I did so now. I forced myself onto two legs and somehow I pushed her back.

I barely made it a single step before she took control of my body. My spine cracking first, the pain was unimaginable as my entire spine twisted and arched, forcing me to the ground. She was determined to be free tonight. I couldn't stop the whimper as every bone in my body broke, quickly and painfully.

I could sense the remaining vampire stalking towards me. Wolf lashed out. We hated being vulnerable. We closed the gap between us and the enemy that was closing in. The creature threw its arms up in defence, but it was no use.

My jaw was still human as it closed around her flesh. We hadn't even hit the ground yet; she never did. She was just a cloud of dust as I collided with the ground. I couldn't stop the cry of pain as my arms and legs began to crack and reform. My whole body was quivering.

All the while I was refusing to give up control to the wolf crushing the edges of my mind. She didn't have control of me yet. As much as I hated it, I forced myself to dive into the cage meant to showcase us to the town. I could sense Agua following me. I sensed the force of the magic as she begun a spell to seal me inside.

A growl escaped my rapidly growing muzzle. That moment of distraction was enough to lose my grip. I felt a whimper escape my body. I had to give Agua as much time as I could. Somehow I pulled back the wolf, muzzle sinking back into my face. I didn't dare move from my curled-up position.

I felt the long deep breaths I was taking, trying to keep her at bay. For the moment the force of the wolf had quelled, but I knew it would be back, and with it even more power. When the next bout started, all I remembered was unimaginable pain as my ribs expanded, I couldn't stop the scream of pain that escaped me and I couldn't stop the onslaught of power she forced upon me as she took over.

I had never experienced such a painful transformation before. Blinded by the pain, I couldn't do anything but retreat to the deepest parts of my mind, but the wolf wouldn't let me have it tonight. She drew me back and forced me to live through every painful moment. Only when the transformation was done did she let me go.

***

All I could feel was the cold and the pain. I shivered, my entire body was trembling as I forced my eyes to open. I was at the base of a tree, I had no idea where. Looking down at myself I could see blood down my chest.

I looked up at the sky. The sun was high, almost noon. I had to get back. I forced myself to my feet, my arm wrapping around my bleeding ribcage. Trying to get my bearings. Gathering my strength, I forced myself to howl. Hopefully someone would hear me. The effort took a lot out of me, my vision clouded and I felt myself collapse even as I was pulled back under.

The next time I woke up I was in a room. I sat bolt upright and I regretted it the moment it happened. I cried out in pain, a hand flying to my ribs. The door opened a moment later and Mira's mother came through.

'Finally,' she said coming to sit by me. I could see the everyday bustling of the hospital in the corridor behind her. 'You've been asleep for ages,' the woman continued, hugging me tightly to her.

I let her hold me, I needed the comfort right then. I opened my mouth to speak. I had to try again. 'What happened?' my voice cracked. 'Why am I here?'

'I needed to work and you needed constant care,' she told me. 'You nearly died.'

'What else is new?' She let out a short laugh. I met her eyes seriously. 'Did I hurt anyone?'

Her gaze faltered and she looked down, submissive. 'Hall's man,' she told me softly. 'He's dead.'

I took in a deep shaky breath. 'Leave me.'

'It wasn't your fault,' she said, getting to her feet. 'The humans know this.' I ignored her and she left. I buried my face into my knees, holding back tears I didn't want to fall. It was happening all over again. Killing a human. I felt sick. How could I face the town after they'd seen what I had done?

'Rya.' I looked up. 'For what it's worth, I'm sorry.'

Anger boiled up within me as I stared at Zac's father. The next moment I was out of the bed and I pinned him against the door. The timber buckled. He cried out in pain. The wolf in me was delighted by the scent of his pain.

'How dare you do this to me?' The growl in my voice was evident. 'I have done nothing to you, and until now I have been nothing but tolerant. You have electrocuted me, put me in a cage, shot me, twice.' Several weeks of anger was bubbling within me. 'If you come near me, my family or my pack again, I will kill you.'

Two sets of arms grabbed me from behind. Pulling me away from Hall.

'You don't want to do that Rya,' Colby said into my ear as the human slid to the floor gasping for breath.

'You have some serious anger management issues,' Hall had the guts to say as he got to his feet.

My lip curled as a snarl ripped out of my throat. Every fibre of my being wanted to kill this man; to kill this human scum. I felt my canines growing in my mouth and my fingers stretching into claws. 'You have made an enemy of me,' I growled. 'Your next move against my people will be your last.' My voice was muffled around my fangs.

I took a deep breath my fangs and claws sinking back to human extremities. I pulled myself out of Colby's grip breathing hard like I had just run a long distance. I took several steps towards the exit. I felt Colby's hand catch my wrist. 'Where are you going?'

'I can't be here right now,' I stated.

He let me go, by "here" he knew I meant the human world. 'Be careful. You're still hurt.'

I knew that, I didn't have to look down to know that my wounds were bleeding through my shirt even as I stood there. Without responding I walked out of the hospital noticing that the humans gave me a wide berth.

On my way out the door I bumped into somebody. Their elbow collided with my ribs causing me to fall as pain spiked through my body.

'Hey, wolfie.' I glared up at Jace. 'I heard you killed somebody.' My breath caught in my chest. I forced myself to my feet and bolted. I was full wolf before I reached the road. I weaved through the oncoming traffic and bolted into the forest. I heard a voice call after me but I ignored it.

I ran deep into the trees, away from the human world. When my aching ribs wouldn't let me run any further I slowed to a walk, my breathing laboured. I knew I didn't have the energy to hunt. I wasn't strong enough to take down a deer on my own and I wasn't fast enough to catch a smaller mammal.

So I settled at the base of a large tree. To regain my strength.

'Rya.' A foreign voice entered my mind. I looked around to find its source. A pitch-black wolf stood not a few metres from me. My first thought was Erik, that the human blood was causing me to hallucinate, which happens by the way.

But then I saw that the black was not the same. Erik had been more of a grey black, while this wolf, this wolf was pitch black, the complete opposite to my pure white fur. He took several steps closer. I edged away, wary of the unknown male wolf, especially while I couldn't fully protect myself.

'Rya it's me,' he seemed to be focusing.

I took in a deep breath, breathing in his scent. He smelt familiar. *'Zac?'* I questioned. His scent was different to what it had been before. His normal sent was tainted by the wolf, by the scent of magic.

His ears flicked back as he came closer. I didn't flinch when his face came into contact with mine. I had forgotten all about him, about him turning into a werewolf. I had only been able to think about…

I took a relaxing breath and he curled up next to me. His wolf was larger than mine and he could easily curl his form against mine. *'How long has it been?'* I asked him, letting my mine meld with his as we curled comfortingly together.

'Dark moon was the night before last,' he answered.

I rested my head on my paws while he rested his on my neck, the tree's trunk at his back. *'How are you?'* I asked softly, I was drifting back to sleep again.

'As good as can be expected I guess,' Zac answered. *'Colby has been teaching me.'* I was barely able to acknowledge his words because I was already falling asleep in his comfortable embrace.

***

When I woke up we were still at the base of the tree, except now we were human and we were naked. His arms were wrapped around me and my back was pinned against his chest. For the moment I forced myself to forget about everything.

I rolled over without waking him curled and in against him. He had survived and now he was one of us. I didn't have to worry about him getting hurt. I looked up at his face. He was so calm, no evidence of the wolf within. The only evidence right now was his scent. It smelt alien to me, nothing like the human boy I cared about so much. It would take me a while to get used to.

He opened his eyes to look at me.

'What?' he asked, with a certain level of affection in his eyes.

'Why aren't you afraid of me?' I asked him. 'Why are you able to be with me now, knowing what I've done.'

'I've never been afraid of you.' I gave him a look. 'Okay maybe I was when I first found out, but then I learned more about you.' I felt myself smile. 'And what you did wasn't your fault. My father did that to you. If you hadn't stayed to fend off the vampires more than one person would be dead now.'

'That's not all of it,' I told him. Curiosity appeared in his gaze. 'When I was little, when I first became a werewolf after my parents died, I didn't know I was going to turn, none of us did.' I took a deep breath. 'I didn't get locked up with my brother and when I turned it was too late to stop me from getting out of the house.' I felt my eyes fill. 'This isn't the first human I've killed,' I admitted, looking down at the ground between us.

His hand went to my cheek, he forced me to look at him. 'Have you ever intentionally killed a human?' he asked me.

I couldn't speak so I gave him the slightest shake of my head. He pressed his forehead against mine. Then very gently he kissed me. 'Then there is no reason for me to blame you.'

I sighed with relief. At least he didn't hate me. Yet. 'We should probably head back before they start to worry,' I told him.

'They were worried the moment they found out what happened and they couldn't find you,' he said. 'Besides didn't you come out here to hunt?'

'I can do that on the way back.' I had more energy today, but my wounds were still bleeding. I forced myself to shift, I really didn't feel like walking naked all the way home.

Apparently neither did Zac because he shifted too. I saw him focusing for a few moments before his wolf shape took hold over him. He kept apace with me as we ran through the trees but I wasn't running fast.

When I reached the usual area the herds liked to graze I slowed down. Within minutes I caught the scent of the herds. I went into hunting mode from there. Instincts took over. I actually forgot that Zac was with me, watching what I was doing, how I was doing it. He knew that at some point he would have to do this himself.

I tracked the herd closer to town. When I reached the area, I found them in a small chasm, safe from almost every side. I stalked towards the edge, moving slowly and silently until I could peer over at them.

One of the deer looked up and ducked towards the ground, hiding behind the brush. After a moment it returned to grazing. I moved closer to the edge and dove at my target, an old buck. The rest of the deer bounded in all directions, startled by my sudden appearance.

My prey however was caught, my jaw still closed over its broken neck bone. It had been a swift kill, hardly any pain. I looked up at Zac. He was crouched on the edge, staring down at me. Hesitantly he got to his feet and jumped down into the chasm.

I used my claws to cut through the skin. The skin of this one wasn't as nice. I indicated for him to try it. I would assume he hadn't eaten the raw meat before. Slowly he leant down and took a grimacing bite of the flesh.

I felt my tail wag slightly behind me as I watched him, first grimacing then tasting it. Finally he found out he liked the taste and he took another bite. I nuzzled into his neck for a moment before starting my own meal, our bodies side by side as we ate.

I could hear something. Talking. I looked up, searching for the source. I didn't like being in this chasm. I quickly ate my fill, Zac was already finished and waiting for me. I bounded towards the wall, leaping off a raised rock. I grabbed the edges of the wall with my claws and pulled myself out.

I paced around, checking the area as I waited for Zac to appear. When he followed my actions, he got as far as grabbing the wall, unused to his canine body he wasn't able to pull himself up. I grabbed his scruff before he could fall and pulled him up.

Movement in the trees caught my eyes. I looked up, eyes narrowing as they focused. There were humans in the trees. School students, and my biology teacher. Right we were studying the local environment, there was an excursion into the forest this week.

They cowered slightly under my gaze, I turned to Zac who was also staring at them and urged him to follow. 'Rya?' I paused mid stride and looked back at my teacher and principal. He had dropped out of the tree.

I could feel the blood around my mouth from the hunt. They had just witnessed me hunting. I turned away. 'Nobody blames you Rya,' he said hurriedly. 'We blame Hall. This death is on his hands.'

'I wish it were that simple.' I was human long enough to say that before I turned back into a wolf and ran off with Zac a step behind me.

I didn't go back to the human world until the next day. Zac refused to leave me so instead I spent the time teaching him. I taught him histories and laws, I found out what Colby taught him and then continued his study, teaching him how to track, which he was pretty good at. I got him to hunt our next meal. Like all first timers it was kind of messy, but he got the job done.

The day I returned to the human world, Colby came into our room at the bunker that morning. He was telling us that we had to get back to the real world eventually. Apparently Zac hadn't seen or talked to any of his friends since the dark moon, he had only been to the hospital with Colby and Toby, and apparently I needed to get back into it too.

He wouldn't take no for an answer so we were soon running to school, all of our stuff still there from dark moon day. I wasn't expecting to find Agua and Toby talking to Hall at the edge of the school.

All the anger I had built up, came rushing back to the surface. 'I want to know where my son is,' Hall demanded. 'Nobody has seen him for days.'

'You mean since you locked us in a cage,' I said flatly, the anger plain in my voice as Hall spun around to look at me. 'Frankly I'm not surprised he didn't call you.' My appearance drew attention from the other students.

He looked first at me, then at Zac. 'I'm sorry.'

'And I really don't give a shit,' I responded. 'Just stay away from us. I already have a desire to kill you.'

'Why don't you then?'

'Three reasons,' I stated. 'First, you're Zac's father; second, I don't want to face the repercussions of tasting your blood, my self-control is already less than it was. If I kill another human it would mean weeks before I would return to normal rather than days.'

'And third?' he asked.

'I'd rather not share my third reason.' There was the slightest hint of a growl in my voice.

'Worried about what people might think?' He teased. I had to remind myself to stay calm. Think happy human thoughts. I pushed past him my jaw clenched to stop from growling.

I sensed his hand the moment before he went to grab me. I grabbed him by the wrist before he could. I twisted, breaking the bone and shoved him to the ground. 'Don't ever think you can touch me,' I stated. 'Try it again and I'll break the other one.'

I continued walking to the door, Zac only a step behind me. We had just reached the door when Hall spoke. 'Zac?' I sensed him pause. 'You're going to stay with her?'

'Last I checked, the pack didn't shoot me with a tranquiliser and put me in a cage for something I had no choice about,' he responded.

'They will never trust you.'

'Trust is earned.' I was surprised that this came from Toby. 'If Rya and Colby trust him, then everyone else will too.'

Mira stepped out of the crowd and stood in front of us. 'The pack is family,' she said. 'Live together, fight together, die together.'

The other werewolves in the school hadn't revealed themselves yet. I was surprised they all did now. Each of them stepping forward even those who hadn't transformed yet and the ones from the middle school. They all flashed their golden eyes, burning through their contacts to reveal themselves. All eight of us.

I looked at each them. They each lowered their gaze as I met their eyes, rightfully submissive. I returned my gaze to Hall, he was on his feet now, staring at the teenagers who had revealed themselves.

'You just hate the fact that Zac doesn't need you anymore,' I said flatly. By the look on his face I knew I'd found the truth. The bell rang overhead. I turned away again and walked into the school, grabbed my books and went to class.

***

I *Ánodos*, or, The Rising was he trial one has to go through to become alpha. Erik hadn't completed the trial, probably because he knew he wouldn't pass. It didn't have to be somebody from the original bloodline; it could be any werewolf. It was just the original family that made the rules, and the ones that implemented them. It was strange knowing that by stepping up to alpha, I was taking up responsibility for the whole of New Jersey.

The older members of the pack took care of the

preparing the clearing. Most of them had attended my father's Ánodos. I knew all about it, mostly because I had known since Damien left that I would go through it myself. I took the time to read every piece of information we had on the ceremony.

It still didn't prepare me for the actual event, or the sight of the clearing when I arrived. Everyone was there already, in human form. There was a pyre. About half way between the centre and the edge, the thirty or so werewolves standing in front of it, a gap in between them, providing a kind of path.

Only one werewolf was standing. Seth - my father's beta. Since he was supposed to have taken up the mantle of alpha after my father died, it was his duty raise me into the position. I walked past the torches that ringed the outer edge of the circular clearing.

I nodded to the werewolves that I hadn't seen since the full moon. Not everybody lived in town. Some of them lived in the surrounding area. Some of them preferred to only interact with the pack when it was necessary, or on occasions like this.

When I reached the red headed werewolf I stopped, turning to face him so the fire was to my right with the werewolves on the left. 'You ready,' Seth asked, his voice was deep.

I nodded. He held out his hand, I held out my arm placing it in his hand. Using a single claw, he cut a long deep wound into the flesh of my forearm. A moment later he did the same to his opposing arm.

We pressed the wounds together, each gripping the others arm. I didn't speak as Seth began to talk.

'Dedoménou óti i epilogí víta aftoú tou pakétou.' As the chosen beta of this pack. *'Tha parachorísei tin exousía tis Álfa eis Rya.'* I bestow the alpha's power unto Rya. *'Kóri tou Jason.'* Daughter of Jason. *'Apógonos tou Lykaon.'* Descendant of Lykaon.

I closed my eyes as the magic washed through me.

TOBY DAVIS

We could all hear the words that Seth was speaking. As he said them, their linked arms began to glow with the same white light from before, the power the Rya had called upon to save Damien. The wind began to pick up, thrashing the trees around in the breeze.

When he finished speaking they stood, silent before the flames, both with eyes closed. Then their arms broke apart. Seth came out of the trance like state, but Rya remained still her arm dropping casually to her side as Seth backed away. His job was done.

The fire began to swirl in the wind, like a tornado of pure heat. The tendril reached out to Rya, spinning around her body. The flames began to dance as they swallowed her, rising until her skin was bathed in their shimmering light. The basic clothes she worn to the ceremony burned away, leaving nothing but bare skin.

Another tendril rose up behind her, reaching over her head towards us. Nobody moved. Everyone waiting. It lashed out, throwing itself around Colby. I shouldn't have been surprised, but then I think I kind of expected to be Rya's beta when she did take up the mantle of alpha.

Unlike Rya, Colby's eyes were open as he was lifted towards the flames. Also unlike Rya he was placed before them, in the place where Seth had been standing. At the same moment, white light shone above the two. Two letters of the Greek alphabet; α and β. The symbol of the alpha and beta wolves.

The symbols disappeared almost as quickly as they appeared, a moment later the bonfire was blown out. When Rya opened her eyes and looked at us, they were glowing, first a bright white before sinking back to their normal golden.

RYA GARCIA

I was crouched on the ground. I felt like my mind had been dug through by thousands of creatures, all at once. I took a deep breath and opened my eyes. The first thing I saw was the pack.

I not only sensed my glowing eyes, I could see the glow they cast upon the werewolves. I felt my body transform, almost of its own will. I could feel my wolf at the edge of my consciousness as her mind began to merge with mine. Now we were one. We would use the best of both sides to run our pack.

We stood up to our full four-legged height. A howl burst forth in our chest and ripped into the silent air. When we looked down at our pack, they were all kneeling. All of them with one knee on the ground, their heads bowed and tilted to the side. The image of werewolf submission. I drew back the wolf, putting her in the back of our mind. She would be there when I needed her.

When I turned my head to look at Colby it was to find him staring down at me, his arms held loosely across his chest. He was the only one that hadn't knelt in submission. As a beta he didn't kneel, he advised. He only averted his gaze from mine, not offering a challenging stare.

Zac was at the back of the group, beside Mira and Brian. It looked like they had pulled him down at the correct moment. He must have sensed my gaze because he looked up as I allowed myself to become human again.

I felt the pang on my shoulder, it wasn't painful, but it was enough to make me look. Light gleamed on the front of my shoulder blade. When it disappeared I was left with three shapes branded into the skin: a circle with two crescents facing inward. The family brand.

When I got to my feet everyone relaxed. The formality was over. I nodded to the werewolves again, they returned the gesture and they all started to leave. Eventually it was only Colby, Zac, Toby and Seth left. Damien and his girl hadn't hung around.

Zac walked over with a fresh set of clothes. I had known mine would disintegrate in the fire. Seth and Colby began walking around the clearing, putting out the torches. Things felt different. Not just that the bridge between me and my wolf was broken. Something else.

I couldn't shake the odd feeling.

'Are you okay?' Toby asked as Zac handed me my clothes.

'Yeah,' I responded, brushing off his concern by getting dressed. Same clothes as before, other than the shirt, this time it was a singlet top, the brand on my skin would remain red and would ache for several days before finally settling down. The last torch was put out leaving us in complete and total darkness.

I laced my fingers through Zac's. 'Let's go. We have training in the morning.'

In the weeks following my rise to alpha the humans treated me differently. In their eyes not only had I killed a human but they were also seeing how I reacted to it. I was more agitated, more on edge. The effects of the blood wore off a few days after returning to school, but I could still feel it in me, I could feel the edginess of my wolf.

I threw myself into training to prevent myself from having a problem. I finished the magic bracelet with Toby and we tested it. After we were sure it worked we made one for each member of the pack. It would take the clothes they were wearing and deposit them into a magic pocket made by Agua, and when they returned to human form the clothes would reappear.

Alec Hall stayed clear. The few times I did see him he had a cast around his broken hand. With the help of Dylan and Sean, Zac moved all of his things into one of the rooms at my house. Damien's old room in fact. He slept in my room most nights but we thought it would be a good idea for him to have his own room and his own space.

The day before the full moon I finally met with Hall, with witnesses. Colby attended from the werewolf side of things, while the Mayor and the Sheriff attended from the town. Everybody in town knew about the meeting.

Colby and I met the three of them at town hall. We sat awkwardly in a boardroom for a few moments before I finally spoke. 'You have questions,' I stated, my voice at normal volume. 'We can give you answers, but only if we want to.'

'So it's official now, right?' the Mayor said. 'You run the pack.'

'Yes,' I admitted. 'I am the alpha. Colby is my beta.'

'Let's pretend I don't know what that means.'

'He's my advisor,' I explained to Richard Fall. Richard had been the elected Mayor for four years now. Nobody opposed him because everybody liked what he was doing. 'Any issues, you can talk to either of us.'

'I have an issue,' Alec said. 'Where's my son?'

'Right now.' I half touched his mind. 'Training with the others.' I admitted in a less then friendly voice. His hand was still in its cast. Good.

'I want him back.'

'He's not yours to have anymore,' I stated. 'He's one of us, he belongs to himself.'

'I don't see the benefits.'

'The pack will support him both financially and emotionally for the rest of his life,' Colby stated, glancing at me. Even my pack had been walking on eggshells around me lately. 'He doesn't have to work a day in the human world if he doesn't want to.'

'You don't seem to mind him as much as others of your kind,' Hall observed.

'I'll admit, I was wary at first,' Colby said. 'But in the past few weeks I got to know him, I've been inside his head. He can be trusted.'

'You were in his head?' Hall questioned. 'How?'

'It's a little talent of ours,' Colby answered. 'We can reach into the minds of those around us.' The three humans suddenly looked worried. 'We can't get into human minds,' Colby said hurriedly. 'For humans, we use body language and emotion.'

'Prove it,' Hall said.

I took this one. 'You want to prove to the world that we're dangerous so they'll lock us up. Then you get to do your research without all this negotiating,' I told him. 'The Mayor wants to understand us. And the Sheriff here is unsure of the entire thing, despite everything that's happened he's still got a slight case of denial.'

'You get all that from body language?'

I nodded. 'Once you read humans enough you get to understand them better.'

'But with other supernaturals we can go straight to the thoughts and memories.'

'I've heard you speak of a bunker?' The last word held a lot of question. 'What is it?' the sheriff asked me.

I glanced at Colby. I didn't really want to show them, but it was the best way to prove we weren't a danger to anybody. He shrugged, I knew he was seeing my train of thought. We couldn't really block each other when we were this close.

'It's probably better if we show you. It's not exactly an easy place to explain,' I admitted.

'Where is this place?' Alec asked.

'You didn't think we would actually tell you that did you?' I reached out to Toby's mind. *'Is Agua still with you?'*

'Yes,' was the response I got.

'Can you send her here?' I asked. *'Warn the others that we're about to have human guests.'* I got brief acknowledgement across the link.

A few seconds later Agua materialised in the room with a brief sweep of the air around her. The humans' reactions were priceless. 'Are you actually going to let him in?' she asked when she closed off the magic.

'It's the best way,' Colby told her. I knew he noticed her look at Hall and her use of the word him.

'I can't carry this many people,' she said after a moment. 'We'll have to go in two lots.'

I nodded. 'Take Colby with you on the first round.'

Without a word, he put a hand around Agua's wrist. I nodded for the Sheriff and the Mayor to do the same. In a blink of an eye they were gone without so much as a sound. A few moments later she rematerialised in front of me.

I grabbed her wrist, my hand closing around it much like Colby's had. When Hall reached towards her wrist she pulled away. Only so he couldn't grab her. Instead she grabbed his wrist. I hid my smirk. She was fine with the others, and judging from the look on Alec's face he knew it too.

I blinked when we were pulled into the void. A moment later I was standing near the entrance to the bunker. I couldn't really imagine what the humans would be thinking right now. The room was huge, full of various equipment. Not to mention the fact there were a few werewolves using that equipment.

'What is this place?' Hall looked amazed as he looked around.

'This is our facility,' I told him. 'We call it The Bunker.' I couldn't help but feel happy over his amazement. 'If you like this, then you'll love the lower levels.'

'There's more?' the Mayor questioned.

'Less listening more training,' I told the werewolves that had come closer. 'Toby work with the bot, start slow and work your way up. Maya, I want you working on that speed, you can be a lot faster.' I looked at Zac, he was trying not to meet his father's eyes. 'Zac work with Mira.' I looked at her. 'Show him course one. Then I want you to run course two.' She nodded. And just like that they were all gone.

I could feel the stares of the humans. 'As you can tell.' I ignored their stares. 'This is our training facility. It's far enough away from the human world that it doesn't matter if the new werewolves lose control.'

'The lower floors are different,' Colby said. He directed them to the stairwell to our right and led the way down.

'Don't stray,' I warned Alec. He was watching Zac as Mira showed him the basic obstacle course. After a moment's hesitation the scientist followed his human companions.

Two flights of stairs later we opened up onto the next floor. 'This is our communications sector,' Colby told them. 'We monitor all police radio and incoming

911 calls across the state.'

'Why?' the Sheriff asked.

'If something supernatural comes up, we deal with it before the cops get to it, or we take over,' I told him. 'Human's aren't equipped to deal with the supernatural, so we do it for them. This state is our territory, so it's our responsibility.'

'How do you monitor so many channels?' Trust the cop to be the one with the questions on this floor.

'We created a program that filters through each communication, and if something comes up the system alerts us,' Colby answered this time. 'We also have access to several satellites across the globe.'

We went down to the next floor. 'This floor is more specialised.' I told them. 'Only certain people are allowed in.'

Instead of the room opening up we were faced with a glass wall. It was glazed so you couldn't see through. The glass was also bullet proof and laced with a compound that even the strongest creature couldn't break through.

'What's in there?' Alec asked.

'That's the area for more specialised training,' Colby told him. 'Only those on the security and defence teams are allowed.'

'It also contains several cells suitable for holding supernaturals,' I added.

We didn't dwell in the closed corridor, leading them down to the next floor. 'This is just residential,' Colby told them, staring down the long corridor. 'There is a mess hall at the end, the store room is stocked with enough food and water to supply us for months.'

The next floor was the one I knew Alec would like. Once again the floor opened up, pillars of stone at various intervals. It looked a lot like Alec's secret lab. 'This is our laboratory,' I told him. 'We have enough workstations for all of us, but there's only a few of us that use this floor.'

'Mostly Rya and Toby,' Colby stated.

'How does nobody find this place?' the Mayor asked.

'It's all underground,' I told him. 'But we've also put magic over the land so it can't be found by technology.'

'What's down there?' Hall asked. He was looking down the next staircase. At the bottom was a large metal door. It was even older and heavier than the one at home.

'More cells,' Colby answered. 'For werewolves in case we ever need to house ourselves out here over a dark moon.'

'That's it,' I told them.

'So do you all live here?' the Mayor asked.

'No,' I said quickly. 'The pack owns a few dozen houses in town, each equipped with the requirements for a werewolf to live without harming anybody.'

We led the way back up to the top floor where the others were still training. Agua was waiting to take us back into town. I sent her back with all three humans. Then she came back for me and Colby.

As soon as we let go of her she was gone. She wanted to get away from Alec, that much I could sense. 'So,' Colby started as we all sat down around the table again. 'What did you think?'

'I never imagined you do all of that,' the Sheriff said.

I laughed. 'It has picked up a little since our location was compromised but other than that, it doesn't take much out of our time.'

'Does this mean we can go on living as we have?' Colby asked the three men.

'I see no problem with it,' the Mayor said.

The Sheriff nodded in agreement. 'Of course some ground rules should be laid down for interactions.'

'Do I get to do my research?' Hall asked.

I sighed. 'I will organise a few blood samples for you; a male, a female and a child.' He opened his mouth. 'I will also organise the basic information about our kind. Abilities, pack structures, reproduction. That should keep you busy for a while. But you only get what we give you and we approve all tests you run.' I stared him in the eyes. 'Got it?' My voice was completely serious.

His broken hand twitched. 'Got it.'

I sat back in my chair. 'Good.'

'Right, well.' The Mayor was looking at me as he spoke. 'Should we organise something to celebrate,' He said. 'Tomorrow night.'

I hesitated. 'Tomorrow's the full moon,' I told him.

'So what,' Colby said. 'I'm sure we can organise something for before sundown.'

'I guess,' I responded. 'But this is the first time the pack will actually enjoy the full moon without worrying about Erik or me.'

The humans were watching us, listening. 'Well ask

the pack,' he said. 'They should have the choice, since it will be revealing them to the town.'

'And if some of them don't want to?' I asked him. 'I won't force them to reveal themselves.'

'They will all do it.' He sounded sure. 'Because it means they won't have to hide who they are anymore. Before you know it, the other packs will reveal themselves too. We have a chance to have the thing we've always wanted.'

'I guess,' I responded.

'Ask them.'

Fine. I didn't have to say this to him because I had already opened my mind to the entire pack. I was glad I didn't have to call or message them anymore, one of the benefits of taking on the role of alpha.

Anyway, I relayed the conversation to everybody. Everyone was pretty much an instant yes, only a few of them were nervous about revealing themselves to the town. Though like me, everyone had been hoping for a relaxed full moon, something the pack hadn't had since my parents died. I told them we shouldn't hang around too long.

'Okay,' I said to the humans in front of me. 'Everyone's on board.' I still had my mind open to the pack, I left it so they could hear what was being planned.

'I was thinking a town camp out,' the Mayor stated.

We did those sometimes. The town would build a whole bunch of fire pits and would camp out under the stars. It was usually paid for with donations from the local butchers and grocery stores, though the city usually gave them some money to pay for the food everybody ate.

I felt the pack cringe. 'As long as we don't have to stay if we decide not to,' I said for them.

'I assume you want me there to translate for you,' Agua said through Toby's mind.

'That wouldn't be a bad thing,' Colby told her.

'That should be fine,' Richard responded, completely unaware that there was a silent conversation going on in our heads.

'We should present the boundaries and rules at this thing too,' the sheriff said. 'Make a town meeting out of it.'

'We won't have time to prepare if we have any actual town meeting,' Richard told Connors.

'Don't worry about it. We will put some of our people on it,' Colby said. 'Rya can stay connected to them so they can hear everything at the meeting.'

'Do you know how hard it is to keep my mind open to everybody?' I asked him.

'You mean you can talk to them wherever they are?' Hall asked.

'Yes,' I answered. 'They are listening to every word we're saying right now.'

He sat back in his chair, arms crossed. 'So much for a private conversation.'

'They've only been listening since we started talking about tomorrow night,' I assured him.

'So I guess we should make those rules then,' the Sheriff put in.

'Our laws remain the same as they always have when interacting with humans,' I told them. 'It's humans interacting with us we need to watch.'

'Why's that?' Hall asked.

'Because humans are often controlled by their emotions and their desires.' I was looking directly at him as I said it so he knew I was talking about him. 'They will often stop at nothing to get what they want.'

There was a full minute of silence while Hall and I glared at each other. 'O...kay,' the Sheriff said awkwardly. He had a pen to paper, ready to write. 'Why don't you tell me what your laws are so tomorrow's meeting doesn't feel one-sided to the rest of the town?'

I could feel the amusement from the pack at the awkwardness I had caused. I closed them out so I could focus on the task in front of me. I started listing our laws when it came to humans. There weren't very many of them.

We spent several hours going over the rules to set for humans. In the end we decided the meeting should be recorded for the news, and the campout out. Though Colby and I drew the line once everyone started falling asleep. As a sign of good faith, Colby and I would stay with the town overnight.

We also planned the day, we made plans for the meeting to be in the morning, and while the town, Colby and I were in the meeting, the rest of the pack would be preparing everything. We wanted it to be more than a camp out. If we were going to do this it would be a way to educate the town about us, on a need to know basis.

By the time we left there that afternoon, the kids of the pack had already started spreading word about the town meeting and the camp out. The posters put up later confirmed everything they were saying. By nightfall the town was practically buzzing with excitement.

'Are you sure you guys want to do this?' the Mayor had asked us as we left the building.

'Let's go with should do this,' I said. 'Not exactly want to.'

'Why?'

'Try to remember we've spent our entire lives in secret,' I reminded him. 'We're about to reveal so much about ourselves to everyone. It's going to change everything,' I continued. 'Not just for our pack but for the others as well.'

'Well I hope it works out,' the Mayor said. 'Your parents were good people. Unfortunately I only had the pleasure of working with them for a short while. I can see that you're just trying to make sure everyone is safe.'

'That's my job,' I reminded him. After a moment I spoke again. 'I will see you tomorrow before the meeting starts.' He nodded and the three humans left.

'So how was your first day of alpha duties?' Colby asked me.

'Shut up,' I said, after a moment we both smirked.

'I'll see you bright and early tomorrow,' he said. 'And no dawdling,' he added.

I laughed. I knew he meant Zac. 'Same to you.' He just smiled as he walked away. I shook my head and turned in the direction of home.

I could feel the effects of the full moon from the moment I woke up. Zac was behind me, his arm loosely wrapped around my body. I hadn't even heard him come in. He had been with Dylan the night before.

When I rolled into him he woke up or maybe he was already awake. I looked over him at the alarm clock on the bedside. I groaned. 'We have to get up.'

'Are we really going to do this whole thing?' he asked me.

He was one of the ones who didn't want to do it.

'We don't really have a choice.' It was more so that nobody had seen him in wolf form yet, not even Dylan or Sean. 'They'll see you as a wolf at some point,' I reminded him.

He looked down. 'I know,' he said. 'But this is going to change everything for me.'

'Yes, it will,' I agreed. Just like with me, knowing Zac was a werewolf, was different to actually seeing him transform. 'Tonight will be painful for you as well.'

'Great.' The sarcasm was thick in his voice. 'Anything else I should know.'

I shrugged. 'Not really.'

I pressed my hand on his chest between us. He always slept shirtless. I knew he felt the same rush of energy that spiked through me, more intense then I had ever felt before. I took a deep breath. I Couldn't do this now, I had to work.

'That's something I don't need to be told about.' I looked up at Zac, I could see the hunger in his eyes, something I had never seen on him before he became a werewolf.

I felt the small smile on my face. 'We have to go,' I said. 'More to the point, I have to go.'

I pulled myself away. It took all my will power to do it though. I pulled my shirt off as I walked to the cupboard. I grabbed the usual tank top and jeans and slipped my magic bracelet onto my wrist. I could feel Zac watching me the entire time. I went into the bathroom and made myself presentable, then I had to leave the house, otherwise I might not arrive on time.

The three humans were already there. Colby wasn't. 'You're late.' Hall stated.

'Give me a break I just woke up,' I responded.

'Where's Colby?' the Sheriff asked. 'He's never late.'

'Probably where half the pack is right now,' I responded. 'In bed.'

'Nope.' The werewolf himself came from nowhere. 'I'm here. It's just a little harder to get out of bed today.'

'How's Lexi taking the reveal?' I asked him as we headed towards the theatre doors.

'Nervous but happy about it,' he responded. 'She's

heading out to round up the others. What about Zac?'

'He doesn't want anyone to think any differently of him,' I said. 'Everyone knows about him but nobody has seen him transform except the pack. Not even Dylan and Sean.'

'He's just scared.'

'Everyone is,' I said, being inside everyone's heads told me that. 'But his fear isn't irrational. Sure, with me everyone's treating me differently because I am different to what I was showing them. I was playing the timid girl who lost her parents,' I said. 'But you didn't change and everyone is treating you differently.'

He didn't answer. The entire town was already filing into seats, all except the werewolves of course. There were two cameras at the back of the hall and two above the stage. All of them were recording. Nothing would be airing until the footage was put together, then it would be aired with footage from today and tonight.

The hall went quiet as the five of us trotted up onto the stage. There were two lecterns on the stage and three chairs to the right-hand side. Richard and I went to the stands and the others went to the seats with the Sheriff in between the werewolf and the scientist.

I opened my mind to all the werewolves of the pack. All of them were either at the park already or on their way there, already setting things up. I glanced at the mayor and nodded, indicating that everyone was listening.

'Thank you for coming on such short notice everybody,' Richard said. 'As you all know, the five of us met yesterday to discuss the revelation of the werewolf population in our town. They let us into their compound and showed us what they do for this town. As a result, Sheriff Connors and I have decided that we can go on living peacefully with them, as they have been living among us without notice for many years.'

He paused and looked at me, indicating for me to continue. I nodded. 'Some of you would know,' I started, 'but I have officially risen to the role of alpha, meaning all werewolves in this town defer to me when it comes to our supernatural lives. Colby,' I gestured at the werewolf behind me, 'is what we call a beta, which means he advises me if I need him to, and stands in if I am unavailable.' I paused. 'If there are ever any concerns about one of our people you speak with me or Colby. Do not confront the person in question as it is our job to keep the pack civil.'

'I don't believe you will have any problems though,' I continued. 'Unless provoked, we are a fairly peaceful people.'

'Which brings us to the main reason for this meeting,' Richard told everyone. 'We have come up with rules and guidelines for when everyone interacts.'

'But not everyone is here!' someone shouted from the crowd. I could not see who.

'But they are,' I said, tapping the side of my head. 'The pack is otherwise engaged right now and aren't attending the meeting. They are however listening to everything we're saying.' I raised an eyebrow. 'Besides you really don't want forty hyperactive werewolves in one room,' I added. 'Instead they're working.'

'Hyperactive?' the Mayor questioned, looking at

me.

I shrugged. 'Full moon effect,' I said. 'It gets worse as the day goes on. Don't worry, no danger, we just have too much energy. By the end of the day we're just waiting to go wolf. Full moon is one of the best days, but it isn't very easy to stand still right now.'

I could feel the excitement of my pack running through me. It was making me almost giddy. 'Anyway, unfortunately all of the rules we made are for the humans of the town,' I told the crowd. The sooner we got through this the sooner I could burn some energy. 'The rules for the werewolves remain the same as they have been for decades. They know the penalties.'

I let Richard handle the rest. The rules were pretty much don't provoke us, don't trespass into pack houses or prevent us from going home on a dark moon. 'We pretty much need to treat them like they are normal human beings,' the Mayor finished. 'These are guidelines more then rules, and we have made them to keep everyone safe. We saw two weeks ago what can happen if you don't follow them.'

I looked away knowing he meant me. I also felt the crowd look at me. They knew he meant me. Right now I was the only one in the pack who had killed a human, and I had killed two of them, not that they knew that. 'I don't remember it and I don't want to know anything about it,' I stated. 'It wasn't my fault but I'm the one who dealt with the consequences.'

The whole room was silent for several moments. I broke the silence. 'Anyway, if we can move on. We are actually done here. But we aren't done with the everything.' The humans looked curious. 'You all know that we have the camp out tonight. The pack will be attending, in wolf form of course. Agua and Jayden Fray will be able to translate whenever needed. Until then though, it's best you get to know us better as werewolves rather than humans,' I told them all.

'My pack has spent this entire meeting preparing the park. There you can learn all the information about us you need to know. You can talk to us, ask pretty much any question, though some we might not answer, but those we do will be answered truthfully.' I paused for a moment. 'And yes, everyone in the pack has agreed to show themselves. They just want a chance to live in the open without being treated differently.' I glanced back at Colby. 'It's what we all want. So please make your way to the park and learn everything you can so you can accept us willingly.' On that note, everybody got out of their seats and rushed for the exits.

I shook my head at their eagerness and started to follow with the others a few steps behind me. When we got there things were in full swing. Werewolves were fighting to burn off full moon steam while humans watched on. There were humans talking to werewolves everywhere.

I took a deep breath. Maybe this was actually going to work. People came up to me, apologised for what Hall did to me, like it was their fault. They asked me questions. Most were pretty basic: how we live, what it's like, humans becoming werewolves, the basic stuff. Nobody talked about my family, to me anyway.

I didn't think anything of it when a helicopter flew over us. I didn't expect somebody to drop out of it. She landed on the ground a few metres from me. Colby who had been standing next to me didn't hesitate.

He grabbed the werewolf and pinned her easily to the ground. Two more werewolves dropped out a second later. 'Stop,' I ordered as Lexi and Keith grabbed them. I looked at Colby. 'Let her go.' After a second's hesitation he obeyed. She didn't leave the ground. I looked at the other two. 'Make a move and my people will put you down.' I glared at them until they lowered their gaze.

'Is that any way to treat your family, Runt?' the woman on the ground said.

I knew that voice. I took a closer look at her. 'Reina?' I questioned. She smirked, the same mischievous smirk. 'I haven't seen you in years.' I held my hand out to her.

She took it and hugged me once she was on her feet, I returned the gesture. 'Hey Runt,' she said. 'I heard you joined our ranks. Where's that crazy brother of yours. I heard he came wandering home.'

Damien appeared out of the crowd then. They greeted each other with a hug. 'What are you doing here Reina?' I asked once it was over.

Her face went serious. 'We heard what you were doing and were wondering if you wouldn't mind a few extras.'

'How many?' I asked.

'My pack,' she responded easily.

'Everyone?'

She nodded. 'Colby here will be happy,' she said.

'Leia is coming.' Colby's face brightened a little. Leia was his oldest sister. She went there after meeting one of the wolves in Reina's pack. 'Don't worry, we'll leave tomorrow. We need to talk.' This last part was silent and was said only to me.

I nodded. 'Okay, but you'll have to hunt. We didn't prepare enough food for your pack as well.'

'Great. I will let the others know to come. The hangar is still in the same place?'

'Like we can move it,' I responded. 'I'll send someone over to open it up for you.

'I'll go,' Keith volunteered. He was staring suspiciously at Reina's two wolves.

I nodded. 'Colby do you want to go with him.' I knew he was itching to see his sister now and he didn't need any further prompting. I looked at my cousin. 'How far out are they?'

'Maybe twenty minutes,' she answered. 'We stopped outside the boundary and sent only one chopper in.'

'Probably a good thing,' I said. 'You should have called.'

'Yeah, well, you didn't give us enough time for that.'

I shrugged. 'Everything has been happening pretty fast lately.'

'We know,' she answered. 'We've been watching. For a while there we didn't think you would succeed in reclaiming the pack.'

'For a while there neither did I,' I admitted.

She smirked. 'So the runt grew up.'

'You seriously need to stop calling me that,' I said,

aware that the humans were listening.

She shrugged. 'You're a few years younger than the rest of us. What else are we going to call you?'

'Maybe my name,' I said.

'You actually have one?' I could sense the sarcasm coming of her in spades. 'I never even knew.'

I shook my head at her. 'Still the same sarcastic kid, huh?' I responded. She elbowed me which got me to laugh. 'Come on I'll show you around.'

Reina looked up at the helicopter. It flew over to an empty area and landed. Three more people got out, two adults and a child. One of the men picked her up and slung her over his back. She looked pretty young. After a moment the helicopter took off in the direction of the hanger that housed our own helicopters.

Once we were close enough, the man put the child down and she ran through the people straight for Reina. She bowed her head in respect to me as the alpha. *'To ónomá moue ínai Katarina.'*

I couldn't help but smile at her. I crouched down, she was so small. *'Eínai oraío na sas gnorísoume Katarina.'* I responded. *'To ónomá moue ínai Rya.* Your mother has taught you well, Katarina.'

'We decided to keep her out of school until she grew a little more,' Reina told me.

I smiled at the girl. 'She's just built for speed.' She grinned at me, such a bright smile. 'You'll be one of the fastest.'

I got back to my feet. Katarina's father was watching me. In the end he held a hand out for me to shake. 'Adam,' he introduced himself.

I shook his hand. 'Nice to meet you. You must be

tolerant if you chose to be with Reina.'

'You probably know better than me that choice has nothing to do with it.'

Our hands fell back to our sides. 'Bitten?' I asked him.

He nodded once. 'I've known for several years now. I decided to turn after we had Katarina.'

'How did you take it?'

'The first year was difficult but I finally feel comfortable in my skin again.'

'Risen to alpha yet?'

He nodded in response. 'A couple of months ago.'

'Then welcome to the family. I look forward to getting to know you and Katarina.'

I looked down as Mika, our youngest, passed me. *'Tha thélate na pernoún to chróno tous mazí mas Katarina,'* she said to the smaller girl. Mika was only a year older.

Katarina looked up at her mother. *'Páo,'* the alpha said. *'Den adéspota.'*

'Mika will take care of her,' I said as the two girls ran to the group of younger werewolves.

I started leading her around the place, introducing her to the Mayor, the Sheriff and Hall. She shook two out of three hands (take a guess which hand she didn't shake). I couldn't hide my amusement.

'What language were you speaking?' Hall asked me. 'Do you have your own language?'

'No,' I said, unable to hide my amusement at his question. 'It was Greek.' He frowned. 'Sometimes things are simple,' I told him. 'Werewolves are Greek. What other language would we speak?'

Reina looked at me. 'So,' she said. 'Think I can still beat you in a fight?'

I smirked. 'Who knows?' I answered. 'It's been so long. We've both changed.'

'Do you want to find out?'

'Maybe later.'

'Getting itchy?'

I shrugged. 'Little bit.' Okay, more than a little bit, I just wanted to rip out of my skin and run. She smirked she knew exactly how much I was holding back. I led her to an empty park bench and we sat down across from each other.

'So how're the rest of them?' I asked.

'They're good,' she responded. 'Eddy's as cocky as ever. I haven't seen the others for a while but as far as I know I'm the only one to rise to alpha so far. Well I was.' She gave me a slight look.

'What happened to your father?'

'Mother was killed a few years ago,' Reina told me. 'He just hasn't been the same since. In the end he decided to step down.'

'I'm sorry.'

'Nah it's okay,' she said. 'I'd rather have him to guide me then have to do this alone.'

'I suppose.' Even I heard the sad note in my voice.

'It must have been hard for you,' Reina said. 'I heard about everything that happened after you turned. You had it pretty rough. Even for one of us. No one thought Erik could be like that. The last time I met him he was one of the sweetest werewolves.'

'Yeah, I remember that side of him,' I told her. 'He was great. I loved spending time with him whenever I went to his house. He and dad were such good friends.'

'Do you know what happened to him?'

'Macy and Jeriah,' I responded.

'Who're they?'

'His mate and his pup,' I answered. 'Jeriah was killed by a human, Macy went a little crazy, killed the human that did it, but it didn't stop. The blood just made her worse. The pack tried to help her but in the end my father had to put her down. She was too dangerous.'

'That actually explains his hatred of humans and your family.'

'Yeah,' I agreed. 'If I didn't hate him so much now, I would feel sorry for him. It shouldn't have had to end with me killing him, but he just wouldn't listen.'

'He killed too many,' Reina told me. 'Humans and werewolves. There was no justification in his kills. The council would have stepped in, but Jerry said we should let you and the pack handle it yourselves.'

'We needed to,' I answered. 'We're stronger, all of us.'

We heard the rustling in the trees before we saw the werewolves. Colby came through first. He was chatting with a dark-haired girl. Standing next to each other, they were definitely related. Upon seeing the girl, several of my pack rushed forward to greet her, hugging her, welcoming Leia home.

I got to my feet as she reached the table with Colby. She looked at me, her face bright and happy, then she knelt, submissive. 'You don't have to do that,' I told her. 'I'm not your alpha.' I was a little self-conscious of the humans staring at us.

She got to her feet. 'You really are just like Jason,' she said. 'He never took part in the formalities either.'

I smirked. 'They aren't always necessary.'

'It's good to see you again Rya.' Then she was ferreted away by Colby as he continued to take his sister to see her old pack mates. I sat back down, seeing Lexi and Leia hug briefly.

Werewolves filtered into the park, one by one. I know the humans noticed the newcomers but they didn't seem any less at ease. But I knew my pack was growing uneasy with so many werewolves from another pack.

Reina and I talked, Damien sat with us for a while, catching up on all the years since we last saw each other. Humans mingled with werewolves from both packs. In my opinion, the day was a huge success.

In the end Colby came and got me about an hour before moon rise. The pack had built the fire pits that morning but now Agua went around lighting them as the sun edged lower to the horizon. 'Are we going to do this?' he asked me.

I nodded. 'Yes. Have them set it up. I asked Agua to prepare it this morning.'

Colby looked over his shoulder and nodded at Keith and Lexi. They had been waiting, but now they disappeared into the forest.

I got to my feet when they returned fifteen minutes later. I hadn't moved for hours, humans had settled on the ground talking easily, but now they followed my movements. My pack followed me they knew they were supposed to follow.

I stopped on a hill. Lexi and Keith were putting

torches into the ground, making a circle around me. The rest of the pack surrounded the circle, the children, including the newly turned werewolves, Mira, Zac, Maya and Toby and everyone that hadn't turned. Only full members of the pack could enter the circled, Damien was in, his girl was not. They ringed the edge, kneeling, their heads down.

Colby walked to stand behind me, to my right, where the beta should be. He was holding a small clay bowl. It was centuries old. There was a red paste sitting in it. 'Toby,' I said, loud enough for the werewolf and the closest humans to hear. 'You may enter the circle.'

He hesitated for a moment under the sudden gaze of the entire town and Reina's pack. He stepped into the ring and walked up to me. He knelt on the ground in front of me, one knee touched the ground, a hand steadying him while his other arm rested on his knee.

'You have completed all the training required of a werewolf in this pack,' I told him. 'Tonight you become a full member of the pack. You will be permitted to attend all meetings and voice opinions on matters concerning the werewolves of New Jersey.' I was speaking down to him. 'Do you wish to continue?'

'Yes,' he responded.

'Do you agree to uphold the laws of this pack, and the laws set by the Wolfen Council?'

'Yes.'

'Do you agree to protect the pack, and its secrets to the best of your abilities?'

'Yes.'

'Will you obey the orders of the current and future alphas of this pack, whomever they may be?'

'Yes.'

'All werewolves are expected to contribute to the pack,' I said. 'Have you chosen how you will do so?'

'Yes.'

'How?'

'I will, contribute to the protection of our lands, our people and the ones who live under our protection,' he said. 'I will become a warrior.'

'This path requires both studying and training. Many of the tasks before you will be more difficult than anything you have faced,' I told him. 'Do you accept the challenge?'

'Yes.'

'Warriors rise,' I said.

Keith, Lexi, Charlie and Charlotte rose from their place in the circle. 'Toby will require someone to teach him the ways of your faction. Who volunteers?'

Keith stepped forward. 'I volunteer,' he said. The others knelt back down again while Keith remained standing.

I nodded at the werewolf and looked back down at Toby. 'Do you accept your teacher?'

'I do.'

Colby held out the paste to me. There was only a small amount, just enough to scoop up with my thumb. Toby lifted his head, I placed my thumb in the middle of his forehead and wiped half of the paste onto him down to his brow.

'Should you pass your blood is one with the pack.' The remainder of the paste went on my own forehead.

I felt the magic filter into my body. My skin grew lighter in the darkening world. Sunset was almost upon us. I took a breath and held my hand out to him. 'Rise.'

Toby clasped my wrist in his hand and I did the same to his as he stood. As soon as he stood straight I felt the glowing magic in my body expand. Toby gasped as it hit him. I knew how he was feeling right now, having gone through it myself. The pain was so much worse then transforming for the first time. Worse then holding the wolf back.

Thankfully it only lasted a few moments. When I could no longer feel the magic Toby straightened, shaking off the pain. 'Welcome to the pack,' I finished. 'Tonight you have the honour of leading the hunt.' I let go of his wrist.

As I said it I saw Reina's pack get to their feet. They wandered towards our pack, mixing in with the locals as the sun sank over the horizon. 'Let's go.' I gestured towards the forest.

Toby didn't hesitate now. He transformed into his wolf form as Reina and her mate reached me. Another werewolf, a female stood, next to Colby. The other pack's beta I assumed. Reina, Adam and I were next, we let our bodies shift. Adam was a reddish grey while Reina's fur mimicked my own, she was slightly bigger though.

Then it was the two betas. After that everyone else followed; the newest were the last to transform. They always were. I watched Zac. He glanced nervously at his friends. They were watching only him now, but he did it. He transformed without making a sound.

Once everyone had turned I looked at Toby and nodded once. He bolted into the trees with near a hundred werewolves on his tail.

***

When the wolves got back to the park it was completely dark. We had full bellies and had burned off some of our full moon energy. I was one of the first to arrive back. I walked silently through the humans, who warily glanced my way, they were sitting around their camp fires with plates of food in their laps.

I stopped at the fire where Agua was sitting, Richard. Dylan and Sean were with her, along with a few other random people from town. I sat down beside the Mayor. I was glad he didn't flinch. Instead he looked at me. 'So what was all that before you left?' he asked me.

'A rite of passage into the pack,' Agua said for me. 'All werewolves go through it once they've completed basic training.'

The Mayor looked at Agua. 'You can understand her, right?'

'Yes,' the witch responded.

He shook his head. 'The world just got a whole lot crazier.'

Agua and I both laughed. Though as a wolf it sounded more like a huff.

I heard it before it tackled me. I ducked my head and the small brown pup sailed over me. I had to catch her before she tumbled into the fire.

She was probably about the size of fully grown Maltese. When I settled back down the pup tried to get me to play with her. She grabbed the fur of my neck, trying to pull me down. I just ignored her. I looked at Agua. 'So what do they think about all of this?' I asked. The witch relayed the message.

'So who is this?' Richard asked instead of answering my question.

'Sophie.' The wolf's ears perked up at her name. 'She's about six months old.'

I swiped the pup away with a paw, holding her to the ground. The pup struggled. I put my face next to hers and gently snapped my teeth. She stopped struggling and stared at me. After a moment I let her up. I laid down on the ground and she laid down between my front paws.

I looked at Agua. They were all staring at me and the pup between my paws. I nudged Agua's mind and she repeated my question again. 'I think it has gone pretty well,' the Mayor responded. 'Other than your cousin turning up, things went to plan. We know more about werewolves now and hopefully we can live peacefully.'

'That would be preferred,' Agua said for me.

'So where's Zac at?' Dylan asked.

I gave a wolf's shrug, but I did touch his mind. He was running. It took me a moment to catch where he was and watch direction he was going in. 'He's on his way back,' Agua said, she must have been looking into my mind, I hardly ever blocked her.

Five minutes later Zac walked out of the trees towards us. Sophie was up and playing again, this time with my tail, which I swished from side to side for her. Dylan and Sean were finding it amusing to watch the playful pup.

I only found out that he was here when he laid down beside me. He didn't look at his friends, but they were looking at him. I was distracted long enough for Sophie to bite my tail. I held back a yelp and looked at the pup.

Without thinking I picked her up by the scruff and carried her away. She didn't struggle. Humans watched me as I passed them to the grey wolf the pup belonged to. Edith was her name. She didn't live in town. She was one of the omegas of the pack, preferring to be alone.

The pup nuzzled her mother but when I turned to leave she tried to follow. Edith caught the pup by the tail and held her back. I walked back to the fire, where the others waited. I laid down next to Zac, paws out in front of me.

All around me werewolves mingled with humans. They obviously couldn't communicate but the kids were helping out where they could, having at least one of them per fire, to translate for the werewolves.

Reina's pack hung back a little, letting the town get used to its resident werewolves. Reina and Adam were curled up together, watching everything like the alphas should but slowly getting comfortable enough to fall asleep.

Zac slowly grew more comfortable and started talking to his friends, with Agua's help. He grew more at ease with them seeing his wolf form. Slowly werewolves and humans started to fall asleep.

Soon it was just us and a few werewolves left. Agua finally claimed to be too tired to continue any longer but I knew she just didn't want to translate anymore. Everyone at our fire started laying down. Colby and Lexi had joined us along the way. They were already asleep Colby curled protectively around the smaller female wolf.

I turned my head at the sound of small paws walking through the grass. Sophie had returned. She crawled into the space between my front paws and curled up into a ball her head resting on her leg.

I nuzzled her slightly with my nose and rested my head on my paws, curling up into a more comfortable position. A moment later Zac moved closer and wrapped himself around me, much like Colby was doing with Lexi. I let myself lean into him and I fell into a peaceful sleep.

I rolled over in my sleep. I could hear the commotion; I opened my large golden eyes as my bedroom door opened. It was mum. 'Hide Rya,' she ordered me. She turned around and faced the kitchen. I watched as her skin rippled with light grey fur. Her eyes momentarily flashed as she called the wolf within.

I jumped out of bed and ran to the window, I quickly looked out the window into the backyard, it was empty, I turned around and looked at the wolf my mother had turned into. She glanced back at me before turning to her attacker. He was a tall man with brown hair and... red eyes.

'Run.' I heard mum shout in my mind. She attacked the man, fangs protruding as she sank them into flesh. I couldn't move as the man easily smacked her against the wall. He grabbed her by the throat, squeezing her windpipe.

'Mum!' I shouted. I growled at the man, but all he did was laugh.

He dropped her to the floor as she shifted back into human form, I didn't need to be told that her neck was broken. He took a step towards me.

'Daddy's dead too sweetheart,' the man sneered. 'He's in the kitchen.'

I felt my intake of breath. I was alone. My brother was

at Colby's house. I finally did what mum told me to do. I ran. I turned around and jumped out the window, I landed in a crouch as I started running on four legs. I was still human but in my panic, I had forgotten to run on two legs.

There was no fence leading into the forest so I jumped off the rocks and bounded into the trees, I could hear the man chasing after me. I was just reaching the street when he caught up to me. He grabbed me by the arm, turning me around, his teeth bared. I screamed in fear.

Lights turned on in houses down the street as I tried to scurry away from him. Doors began to open and light fell upon his face. He glanced briefly at the people that appeared, then smiled at me. 'Looks like you get to live sweetheart,' he whispered. Then he was gone.

***

I half lurched into consciousness, sitting up where I was on the ground. I closed my eyes, leaning my head in my hands as my heartbeat settled. I flinched slightly when a hand touched my shoulder. If I hadn't immediately sensed who it was I would have pinned Colby.

I gave him the slightest nod. Silently telling him that I was fine, but I couldn't help but sense the worry of the people that surrounded me. Apparently I was the last one in our circle to wake up, except for Zac. he was awake now though, stretching as he yawned.

I could feel the usual sickness in me that usually came with the full moon, but there was something else.

'Something's not right,' I told Colby.

'What do you mean?' he asked me.

The circle of humans was listening intently. 'I don't know, but I have a really bad feeling.'

I felt myself shiver as wolf bristled within me. Something was very wrong. A moment later a hoard of vampires bolted out of the trees, but that wasn't what caught my attention. The air swirled in a mini tornado right next to the burnt-out fire pit.

I saw who it was before they had fully appeared. Seven years of anger bristled within me, as I forced myself to my feet. The vampires were already being taken care of by various werewolves from both packs. The humans were either staying still or running for safety.

When the man from my dream looked at me, my only reaction was to growl, a deep threatening growl. My wolf echoed me. She was desperate to get a piece of him. 'I had wondered if you would remember me,' he said in a sarcastic drawl.

'How could I forget?' My voice showed just how close I was to transforming and ripping his throat out.

'I'm not here to kill you sweetheart,' he said. 'You're still useful to me.'

'I would never help you,' I growled. 'I want nothing more than to tear your heart out of your chest.'

'Yes,' he said, sounding delighted. 'I did hear you're a little closer to the wild side, is this one or two humans now? Best not get a third, I hear wolves are impossible to control after the third.' He smiled. 'No, I'm here to offer you a deal.' I waited. 'Come with me and I will spare the life of your mate.'

I looked behind me. Three vampires were holding

Zac down, another had a hand wrapped around his throat. Nobody was close enough to help. 'What do you want from me?' I asked, aware that the humans who were close enough were listening to the two of us.

'I want your help,' he said. 'Your great grandfather hid something from me, the information is passed down through your bloodline.'

'In case you forgot, you killed my father before he could teach me anything,' I told him. 'If my family hid something from you then there was a good reason. I will never help you. It is my duty to keep the balance.'

'Then your mate dies.'

'No one life is worth disrupting the balance. Everything we've worked for would be destroyed.'

'How very noble of you,' he sneered, like he knew I would say something of this sort. 'You're definitely Jeriah's granddaughter.' My eyes narrowed at my four times great grandfather's name.

Lexi and the twins were sneaking up behind him, in wolf form. 'How do you know Grandfather Jeriah?' I asked. 'He lived nearly three hundred years ago.'

'We have our history,' the creature teased.

I fought the urge to growl, and instead I glanced at Zac. Colby was circling them, trying to find a way to Zac, his muzzle was slick with blood from previous fights. 'I'll make you a deal sweetheart,' the man said, redrawing my attention. He was closing the distance between us.

'What's that?' I could hear the doubt in my own voice.

'Come with me and I will leave your precious town alone.'

My eyes narrowed, we were less than a metre apart now. 'How about no.'

I closed the distance between us, skin melting around me as I attacked. I pinned him to the ground and closed my teeth around his throat. I barely drew blood before he disappeared. I sensed him the moment before he struck and I leapt out of the way. I turned and dove in grabbing his leg and tearing through flesh with my teeth.

His skin shimmered as the pain ran through him. Wait… it shimmered, like with fur, like us. I would force him to reveal himself. I jumped back as he slashed at me with clawed fingers. I immediately leapt forward again, grabbing him anywhere I could with my fangs causing as much pain as possible.

I managed to get a grip on his shoulder just as I was thrown away. Skin and muscle came with me and the murderer screamed out in pain. I hit the ground, a whimper escaping my mouth as I flipped over the ground, losing my wolf form before I stopped.

I looked up at him. He looked half way between two forms much like us. He was a shape shifter of some kind. His muzzle elongated, large sharp canines protruding from the formed jaw. His muscles bulged and ripped through his clothing, his eyes turned a solid golden yellow, just like a werewolf's.

He growled as he took to four legs, the vibration of it shook my bones. Before my very eyes he turned into the largest white wolf I had ever seen. He would have easily been twice my size.

Oh shit. I thought to myself. The large wolf turned towards me another growl rumbling through its throat. Without hesitation I growled back, my human vocal cords vibrating to create the animalistic sound.

I leapt forward to make the first move, my body changing once again to become a wolf. When I reached the other canine, he was ready for me. I feinted left the leapt right before closing in for the attack. I could feel my wolf sitting at the edges of my mind, she knew we couldn't win this. That didn't stop me from trying though.

Every time I attacked, the wolf would grab me with fangs or claws and force me away. My self-control was slowly waning as my wolf came closer to the surface. My most recent impact was so hard that I broke my hind leg, the snap vibrating through my body as I collapsed in pain and returned to human form.

I held a hand to the wound on my leg, the bone was protruding from the skin. I gasped, my vision fading slightly as it throbbed. I positioned my hand, vaguely aware that my opponent was closing in on me.

Without a second thought I repositioned the bone with a crack and a cry of pain. I turned out of my sitting position, my body coated in dirt and sweat. I took a deep breath, no holding back. I reached in to the deepest parts of my mind and let go.

COLBY MARTIN

With Toby's help I had managed to free Zac from the three vampires' clutches. Now all we could do was watch as Rya fought the creature who had murdered her parents. 'Why don't you help?' the mayor had asked at one point.

'This is her fight,' I answered.

Though I was about to leap in when she hit the ground and broke her leg. Without the full use of her hind leg she wouldn't have as much power. Instead all I could do was watch as the gigantic wolf closed in on her.

Then something happened I wasn't even sure what. Her back was to me as she faced the giant wolf. I couldn't see her face but I could see the alpha marking on her back as it began to glow. It shone brighter and brighter. At the same time the sky above us began to darken.

Lighting flickered through the sky and the rest of Rya's skin began to glow. Before my eyes I saw the wounds on her body begin to heal, the larger wolf hesitated when Rya reached up with her hand. Lightning struck, I heard her growl of pain as the electricity rushed through her. When the lightening stopped she pointed at the large wolf.

The electricity rushed out of her body and struck the wolf before her. He dodged at first, leaving scorch marks in the ground where he had been, but he wasn't fast enough to avoid her. He crumpled to the ground as the lightning struck for a second time.

When it stopped, Rya rushed forward, the glow of her body returning to normal as she leaped into canine form. I could see her just enough to see that her eyes continued to glow a blinding white as she rushed towards the injured wolf. Somehow it managed to dodge out of her way and it turned back into the original human form. Before Rya could attack again he disappeared and he didn't reappear.

Slowly I got to my feet and walked towards her. The wolf was looking around, as if the man would reappear at any moment. It was making me edgy. When I reached her, she looked directly at me, as if trying to remember who I was.

'Be careful,' I heard Reina shout out to me. 'One wrong move and she can kill you.'

I knelt down on the ground in front of the wolf. Feeling the alpha's dominant gaze upon me. slowly I lowered my head in silent submission. 'She would never hurt us,' I responded, glancing up briefly at Rya before looking down again. I didn't realise that the rest of our small pack of thirty or so werewolves had mimicked me, kneeling in submission, as their alpha looked at them.

I reached my hand out to her, palm forward. Her white eyes stared at it for a moment, then she pressed her forehead into my palm, when she reopened her eyes they were back to normal for only a moment before she collapsed.

RYA GARCIA

When I woke up I was alone in my bedroom. When I tried to move, all I felt was pain rushing through me. Despite the constant pain I forced myself upright, reaching out with my senses. There was nobody in the house at all.

I managed to walk to the bathroom where I stripped and turned on the water in the shower. Using the basin for support I inspected my body. I could see no damage to my skin at all, no cuts or even bruises. My skin felt raw. When the water was finally hot I used it to soothe my aching muscles.

I watched as the water had a tinge of brown as the dirt washed away along with the dried blood. I turned slightly and hissed in pain. The water had hit my alpha brand. Gritting my teeth, I forced myself to stay under the water until I was clean.

I was careful not touch the mark with the fabric as I pull my clothes on. I wore a tank top to avoid any extra pain. With some effort, I walked out of the house into the forest, heading in the direction of town, I didn't have the strength to hunt, I didn't think I even had the strength to transform. It was hard enough to focus my senses.

When I walked out of the forest the park that had been so full of people was now empty. I couldn't see anybody. I walked into Kraze and took a seat quietly in the back corner. After a brief scan of the room I confirmed that there were no pack members in the restaurant.

The waitress came over and took my order. She looked shocked to see me but went to get a rare steak and chips for me to eat. When she came back I ate silently in my corner, ignoring the glances of the few patrons in the building.

My strength somewhat returned with the almost raw meat but it was nowhere near as effective as freshly killed meat. I was nibbling on my chips when people I knew came in. It was Colby and Zac. They didn't see me at first; they looked worried. When they scanned the room they saw me, huddled in the corner with my knees folded up in front of me.

Within moments they were sitting on either side of me. 'What are you doing here?' Colby asked me.

'Eating,' I responded. My voice cracked slightly. 'I don't have the strength to hunt.'

'You should still be in bed,' he told me.

'No,' I retorted. 'I need to get back on my feet and train to defeat that stupid thing.' I could feel my rage boiling. He had gotten away from me. It was my chance to avenge my parents and he got away.

'I don't think he will be back for a while,' Colby told me. I knew he could sense my brimming anger. 'But at least wait until you're strong enough to train.'

'Fine,' I conceded. I was planning on starting the next

day, whether Colby liked it or not.

A group of people came in to the restaurant then. It included Zac's friends, Agua and Toby. When they saw me they rushed over to our table. They bombarded me with questions and I couldn't focus on any of them, though I think it was a mixture of "how are you feeling" and "what happened out there." My mind couldn't take it right now. 'Just stop, okay!' I shouted. The entire room went silent as I ran my fingers through my hair.

I took that as my cue to leave. I forced myself past Colby and walked towards the exit. I was about to walk out the door when a wolf came running towards it. It had come out of the forest across the road.

This wolf was different though. It had a cylindrical pouch attached to its back, with the cylinder resting across its back. I stopped when I halted in front of me. This wasn't a familiar wolf. It kept its head down as it returned to human form.

'Alpha Rya,' the wolf said, its voice and body submissive. 'I bare a message from Lupus.'

I felt the surprise cross my face, but I quickly hid the emotion. 'I thought we were past messenger wolves?' I said with a smile. 'I have a phone number.'

The wolf smirked. 'Apparently not for official matters.'

'And the message?' I asked.

He reached over his shoulder into the pouch pulling out a piece of rolled up paper. 'You're invited to the next meeting of the Wolfen Council, the details of when and where are enclosed. Lupus said it's about time your pack joined the war.'

I nodded. 'Thank you,' I said. 'Feel free to freshen up

at the bunker before you head back to the council.'

He nodded his thanks and ran back into the forest, turning back into his grey wolf as he went. I made the paper flat and folded it before putting it into my pocket. I started to follow him; I wanted to relax in the trees for a while.

I don't even know what happened next, I could just feel burning all over my skin. I barely had my eyes open. I forced them open now. I was covered by some sort of metal net. But every time I tried to move my skin began to sizzle.

The rest of the werewolves were still inside, so it took them a moment to realise that something was happening. By that time the net was being lifted into the air by… I think it was a helicopter… I didn't want to move and have the net break the skin.

I saw Colby break into a full run on the ground below me. He jumped up onto the roof of buildings, he used these to reach us before we gained too much altitude. He grabbed the metal and I felt a sudden dip in the chopper above us. But he held on for only a moment before the metal burned him.

The pain forced him to let go. At first he fell backwards towards the ground below, in the last few moments he flipped over to land on all fours as he turned wolf. Without a second thought he raced after us.

Now that my captors had lost the extra weight, we rose higher and higher into the sky, until Colby was just a speck on the ground below. Then we flew over a mountain and he was gone.

To be continued…